POP CORN PIMPS

POPCORN PIMPS
June, 1996.

File under: Good-natured humor diguised as filthy pornography / cartoons

POPCORN PIMPS is published by Fantagraphics Books and is ©1996 Pat Moriarity.

ISBN: 1-56097-254-8

All characters, stories and art are ©1996 Pat Moriarity and his disrespected collaborators:
Dennis P. Eichhorn, Joe Hoppe, J.R. Williams, Mike Campbell, Mike Lang, Aesop,
2-live Crew, Jim Blanchard, Art Penn, and especially Dennis Worden.

Editorial assistance by Gary Groth, of all people.

Covers, design and color by Pat Moriarity.

Endpapers by Jeff Johnson & Pat Moriarity.

Most of this material is reprinted from a variety of interesting sources, all of which are listed
in the table of contents. No part of this book may be reproduced without written permission from
Fantagraphics Books or the creator(s).

No similarity between any of the names, characters, persons, and institutions in POPCORN PIMPS
and those of any living or dead persons is intended, and any such similarity that may exist is purely
coincidental, with the rare teeny exception of biographical and autobiographical material.

Letters to POPCORN PIMPS can be directed to:

Pat Moriarity
c/o Fantagraphics Books
7563 Lake City Way N.E.
Seattle, Washington
98115

First Printing: June, 1996.

Printed in beautiful Canada.

If you liked this book, check out Pat's outstanding comicbook series,
BIG MOUTH, now in its sixth issue from Fantagraphics books.

This book is for you and you only.
Keep it away from kids and potential criminals, because we all know
how material like this can cause terrible, unthinkable crimes.

introduction
By Dennis P. Eichhorn

Partners in crime, left to right: Pat Moriarity, Dennis P. Eichhorn, J.R. Williams and, uh, Jim Blanchard.

I first met Pat Moriarity when I was scripting the early issues of Real Stuff for Fantagraphics Books. On one of my occasional visits to their hallowed studios in Seattle's north end, I was approached by Pat, who had recently been hired as an assistant art director. He displayed his recent autobiographical cartoon work, and halting and self-effacingly offered to collaborate on a story with me.

The moment that I viewed Pat's sequentialistic efforts, I knew that I was in the presence of a seriously deranged but tremendously gifted artist... plus, he was willing to work for virtually nothing! That's an unbeatable combination in the alternative comic book business, and this was obviously an opportunity that begged to be seized!

Pat and I batted some story ideas around, and the upshot was his carefully crafted "Death of a Junkie" in Real Stuff number four. This was followed by several other collaborative ventures, each one better than the last.

It's been a real pleasure to watch Pat's artistic talents flourish and advance. Working at Fantagraphics, he's been in a perfect position to closely examine the stellar work of the world's top graphic artists, and he's incorporated aspects of their styles and techniques into his œuvre.

And what an œuvre it's becoming! Big Mouth comix has emerged as a truly unique and exiting compendium of cartoon interpretation, as Pat has artfully rendered the scripts from a pantheon of creators in his own inimitable manner.

But some of Pat's finest work hasn't appeared in Big Mouth. He's a prolific free-lance cartoonist and illustrator, as this collection amply attests. These are Pat's outtakes... and they are in a class all by themselves.

Simply stated, Pat Moriarity is one of the most innovative illustrators to ever work in the cartoon medium... and he's getting better all the time! It's been an honor to collaborate with him, and I hope to continue doing so for many years to come.

contents

Popcorn Pimps
from Graphic Story Monthly
1

A Bit on Naughty Bits
from Roberta Gregory's Naughty Bits
15

Death of a Junkie
from Dennis P. Eichhorn's Real Stuff
16

Moriarity Mouse
from Pictopia
22

The Man with Two Mistresses
from Aesop's Fables
23

True Story
from Pictopia
27

Oregon Chainsaw Massacre
previously unpublished
28

Me So Horny
from 2 Live Crew's anti-censorship comic
30

A Love Fantasy
previously unpublished
32

The Pathetic Worm
in "He Whom We Abuse"
from Dennis Worden's Cruel and Unusual Punishment
34

Composer's Block
from Jim Blanchard's Bad Meat (and Screw Magazine)
36

Thanksgiving with Maggie Bloodstone
from Naughty Bits
39

Fuss on the Bus
from Dennis P. Eichhorn's Real Schmuck
40

Frank Lloyd Wright is So Mundane
from Shary Flenniken's Seattle Laughs
42

Proof
from The Amazing Adventures of Ace International
44

On the Road With the Goops
originally published in a 45 rpm record package
47

Celebrity Car Crash Corner
from Roger Corman's Death Race 2020
55

Mr. Statistic Moves to Seattle
from Seattle Laughs
56

Duck Blood Soup
from the Northwest Cartoon Cookery
58

How the Comics Journal Gets Made
from The Comics Journal
59

Devil Stay Away From Me
originally a Starhead mini-comic
60

Karmic Kegling
from boing boing Magazine
62

Dig the New Breed!
previously unpublished
64

The Human Blockhead
from the WFMU calendar 1996
66

pop•corn pimp (pop´kôrn´ pimp), *n.* **1.** police slang term for any low priority criminal, falling to the wayside in favor of the more dangerous ones. **2.** such criminals when popped. [short for *popped corn pimps*]

POP CORN PIMPS
OKAY, HERE WE GO. I'VE GOT TO GET THIS OFF MY CHEST. I'VE BEEN LOOKING FOR AN EXCUSE TO DRAW SOME SORT OF CARTOON STORY (MY FIRST) AND NOW I HAVE A STORY TO TELL!
I'M GOING TO BASE THIS STORY ON TWO STATEMENTS TAKEN ON AUGUST 11TH AND 12TH, 1987 IN THE ROBBERY DIVISION, MPD, CITY HALL IN MINNEAPOLIS AND ON A FRONT PAGE STORY FROM THE ST. PAUL PAPER ENTITLED...
Drug-related scam terrorizes motorists who help a stranger
©1988 PATRICK MORIARITY
SO, WHAT'S THIS ALL ABOUT? WELL, I WAS ONE OF THOSE MOTORISTS, PROBABLY THE FOURTH VICTIM OUT OF THE 10 OR 15 CASES INVOLVING THE SAME MEN, AND I WANT TO RECOUNT MY CASE. WHY? I WANT TO WARN OTHERS, AND I GUESS IT'S SOME SORT OF SELF-CATHARSIS' THING. IT'S A CHANCE TO COMPLAIN ABOUT THE HANDLING OF THE CASE AND EXPRESS A NEW LACK OF FAITH IN THE JUSTICE SYSTEM.
THAT'S ME MAKING MY STATEMENT LAST SUMMER. BEFORE THIS STARTS I WANT TO MENTION THE FACT THAT THE SUSPECTS HAPPENED TO BE BLACK. DON'T TAKE THIS AS A RACIST STORY. ANY PERSON OR PERSONS COULD BE IN THEIR SHOES OR MINE... ANYWAY, HERE'S HOW IT WENT
NAME, AGE, DATE OF BIRTH?
PATRICK D. MORIARITY 26, 6/17/61
TAP
TAP
TAP
THE CONSTITUTION REQUIRES I INFORM YOU THAT BLA BLA BLA... ANYTHING YOU SAY CAN AND WILL BE USED AGAINST YOU BLA BLA IF YOU CANNOT AFFORD A LAWYER BLA BLA DO YOU UNDERSTAND EACH OF THESE RIGHTS AS I HAVE EXPLAINED TO YOU?
YES
INVESTIGATOR SGT. STREAM
DO YOU WISH TO TALK TO ME AT THIS TIME AND MAKE A FORMAL STATEMENT?
YES
CALLING YOUR ATTENTION TO 8/8/87 AT APROXIMATELY 0900 HRS, WHERE WERE YOU?
TAP
TAP
TAP
ON SATURDAY MORNING, AUGUST 8TH, 1987 AT 9:00 I WAS AT THE FILLING STATION ACROSS FROM MY HOME GETTIN' GAS AS I WAS LEAVING TOWN.
Antique's wholesale
OPEN
OOM!
Q: IN YOUR OWN WORDS CAN YOU DESCRIBE TO ME WHAT HAPPENED AT THAT TIME?
A: I WAS HEADING BACK OUT TO MY CAR WITH MY COFFEE WHEN I CAME ACROSS TWO BLACK MALES WHO WERE WALKING AROUND IN THE PARKING LOT SAYING THINGS LIKE "HOW 'ZIT GOIN? WUT 'ZAPPEN? WHERE YA GOIN?" THEY WERE PRESSURING ME FOR A RIDE.
INSTANT CASH
REALLY? WE'RE GOIN' UP NORTH TOO. JUS' NORTH MINNEAPOLIS, THO. SAY, HOW 'BOUT A LIFT? WE JUS MISS' THE LAS' BUS.
WELL...
I WAS HEADLONG ON MY WAY NORTH TO DEER CREEK TO SEE JEFF OLSON, AN ARTIST BUDDY WHO WAS ANXIOUSLY WAITING FOR ME TO SHOW. BUT THESE TWO GUYS WERE BEGGIN' AND BUGGIN' ME SO MUCH AND GETTING ME IRRITATED THAT I FINALLY CONSENTED TO GIVE THEM A RIDE TO NORTH MINNEAPOLIS JUST TO GET THEM OFF MY BACK. I NEVER SHOWED.

SHOWING YOU A PHOTO LINE-UP OF 8 ADULT BLACK MALES— DO YOU RECOGNIZE ANY OF THESE MEN?
NUMBER 4 AND NUMBER 7 —THESE ARE THE ORIGINAL TWO THAT HARASSED ME AT THE FILLING STATION.
NOT THEM AGAIN
FOR THE RECORD, THE VICTIM HAS IDENTIFIED PHOTO #4 WHICH IS THAT OF LEXY SMITH, AND PHOTO #7 WHICH SHOWS THE NAME DARREN SMITH. THESE PHOTOS HAVE BEEN SIGNED BY THE VICTIM AND BY SGT. STREAM.
4
7
Q: WOULD YOU DESCRIBE TO ME WHAT HAPPENED SUBSEQUENT TO YOUR CONSENTING TO GIVE THESE TWO BMs A RIDE TO NORTH MINNEAPOLIS?
A: WE WENT ON UP TO NORTH MINNEAPOLIS, WENT DOWN AN ALLEY, AND STOPPED AND THIS WAS WHEN I EXPECTED THEM TO GET OUT SO I COULD BE ON MY WAY.
THIS IS WHEN THIS "LARRY" OR WHOEVER (PHOTO NO. 7) WENT INSIDE A HOUSE AND "DEE" (PHOTO NO. 4) WOULD NOT GET OUT OF THE CAR AND I TOLD HIM THAT I WAS IN A HURRY AND THAT I WANTED HIM TO GET OUT SO I COULD BE ON MY WAY.
COM'ON! A FAVOR'S A FAVOR I GOTTA GO!
"DEE" TRIED TO REASSURE ME THAT "LARRY" WOULD BE RIGHT BACK AND THAT THEY JUST WANTED TO BE DROPPED OFF AT A QUICK BURGER PLACE NEAR BY AND SOON I'D BE OFF FOR DEER CREEK.
OH JEEZ, THIS SOUNDS LIKE A DRUG DEAL... JUST DROP THEM OFF AT THE BURGER PLACE AND GET THE HECK OUTTA HERE!
AT THIS TIME "LARRY" CAME BACK OUT WITH ANOTHER GUY ("STEVE") AND NOW I HAVE 3 OF THEM IN MY CAR. AT THIS POINT I KNEW THAT I HAD GOTTEN MYSELF INTO A BIG MESS AND I FELT THAT I HAD LOST CONTROL OF THE SITUATION — I SHOULD SAY I KNEW I HAD LOST CONTROL...
THEY TOLD ME TO DRIVE TO A BURGER PLACE LOCATED NEARBY ON A BUSY STREET, WHICH I DID, BUT WHEN WE GOT THERE THE GUYS WOULD NOT GET OUT OF THE CAR!
!※#☆?!
ZOOOOM!
WE GOT INTO AN ARGUMENT AND WHEN THEY REALIZED THAT I WASN'T GOING TO COOPEPATE, THEY STARTED TALKING LIKE THEY HAD THINGS TO DO AND IF I WASN'T GOING TO HELP THEY PRETTY MUCH TOLD ME THAT IF I DIDN'T COOPERATE THEY WERE GOING TO DO IT ANYWAY. THAT'S WHEN THE FORCE STARTED.

Panel 1: "DEE" GOT OUT OF THE CAR, WALKED AROUND TO THE DRIVER'S SIDE AND TOLD ME TO GET OUT, THAT HE WAS GOING TO DRIVE MY CAR. AT THAT POINT HE PULLED ME OUT OF THE CAR AND JUMPED INTO THE DRIVER'S SEAT.

Panel 2: "LARRY" GOT INTO THE FRONT SEAT OF THE CAR AND, IN AN ATTEMPT TO BE FORCEFUL BUT REASSURING, (YA KNOW, LIKE BLACKMAIL?) URGED ME TO GET INTO THE CAR BECAUSE THEY HAD THESE THINGS THAT HAD TO BE DONE AND IF I'D COOPERATE, IT'D TAKE A SHORT TIME AND I'D BE ON MY WAY. OTHERWISE....

Panel 3: THIS WAS APPROXIMATELY 1000 HRS. I WAS STANDING IN THE PARKING LOT THINKING ABOUT WHETHER OR NOT I WAS GOING TO LET THEM STEAL MY CAR... (I JUST BOUGHT IT THAT WEEK... NOT IN MY NAME YET.... NOT INSURED YET!) I DECIDED TO GET INTO THE CAR.

Panel 4: AS SOON AS I STARTED INTO THE BACKSEAT, THIS "STEVE" REACHED OVER, GRABBED MY ARM, PULLED ME IN AND REACHED AROUND ME AND LOCKED THE DOOR. "DEE" TOOK OFF.

Panel 5: "DEE" WAS DRIVING AROUND AND THEY WERE TALKING TO EACH OTHER ABOUT WHAT THEY WERE GOING TO DO. "LARRY" WAS KIDDING AROUND ABOUT HIS EAR... PART OF IT WAS BITTEN OFF.
"SO THAS' JUS' WHAT HAPPEN THE LAS TIME I LIED TO SOMEONE. YOU DON'T BELIEVE ME?"
HAW HAW!

Panel 6: HE THEN OPENED THE GLOVE BOX AND FOUND MY CHECKBOOK AND THEY WERE ALL AT ONCE ASKING ME IF I HAD ANY MONEY.

Panel 7: I STUPIDLY PULLED OUT MY BILLFOLD AND "STEVE" GRABBED MY WALLET AND OPENED IT AND TOOK OUT $25.00 AND THIS IS WHEN "STEVE" SAW MY CASH CARD AND MY PAYROLL CHECK. THEN THEY STARTED WITH THIS STORY THAT THEY HAD TO GET SOME MONEY TO GET SOMEONE A PLANE TICKET TO KEEP HIM FROM GOING TO JAIL AND TOLD ME THAT I MUST TAKE MONEY OUT AND TOLD ME THAT IF I DIDN'T THEY WERE GOING TO "KICK MY ASS" AND THAT ONE OF THEM WOULD BE GOING IN WITH ME TO OBTAIN THIS MONEY AND MAKE SURE I DIDN'T SCREW ANYTHING UP.
TAP TAP TAP

Panel 8: DID YOU FEEL AT THIS TIME THAT YOU WERE FREE TO TAKE YOUR CAR AND LEAVE?
NO, I FELT THAT I WASN'T FREE TO LEAVE AS SOON AS I WAS I PULLED FROM THE DRIVER'S SEAT.
DID YOU FEEL THREATENED AT THIS TIME?
YES, I FELT THREATENED BY THE FACT THAT I HAD 3 BLACK MEN IN MY CAR PRESSURING ME TO COOPERATE OR GET HURT.

Panel 9: Q: WOULD YOU PLEASE CONTINUE WITH THE SUBSEQUENT EVENTS?
A: THEY DROVE ME TO AN INSTANT CASH MACHINE AND TOLD ME TO GET IN THERE AND GET THEM $100. ALL THREE WERE THREATENING THAT IF I DIDN'T DO WHAT THEY TOLD ME, THEY'D TAKE OFF WITH MY CAR — BUT NOT WITHOUT SEEING ME HURT FIRST.
HELLO

Panel 10: FOR THE RECORD, THE VICTIM HAS GIVEN SGT. STREAM A QUICK CASH CARD AND A RECIEPT FROM A QUICK BANK. WITHDRAWING $100 FROM LOCATION BLA BLA... AND LOCATION BLA BLA... THIS WILL BE PROPERTY INVENTORIED BY SGT. STREAM.

Panel 11: Q: AFTER LEAVING THE QUICK BANK LOCATION 2127, WHERE WERE YOU TAKEN?
A: WE WENT STRAIGHT BACK TO THE ORIGINAL HOUSE DOWN THAT SAME ALLEY. "STEVE" AND "LARRY" BOTH WENT INSIDE AND IT SEEMED I WAITED THERE AN ETERNITY WITH "DEE". HE WAS AT THIS TIME IN THE BACKSEAT WITH ME TRYING TO KEEP ME CALM AND SITTING CLOSE ENOUGH TO PREVENT ME FROM GETTING OUT.
NOW LOOK MAN JUS' STAY COOL AND NOTHING BAD WILL HAPPEN

Panel 12: I KNEW BY THEN THAT THEY WERE BUYING DRUGS AND THEY BEGAN SMOKING CRACK, A HIGHLY ADDICTIVE AND CONCENTRATED FORM OF COCAINE, IN THE CAR CONSTANTLY AFTER.
(LOOK, I'M NO SAINT, BUT YOU'D HAVE TO BE CRAZY TO SMOKE CRACK OR IT MAKES YA THAT WAY ANYWAY, PROB'LY.)
GLASS TUBE WITH SCRATCH-PAD CHUNKS AND CRACK PELLETS

Q: WHERE DID YOU GO AFTER YOU LEFT THE ALLEY?
A: I WAS THEN TAKEN TO MANY PLACES WHERE WE STOPPED & LEFT AND I WAS TOLD TO CASH CHECKS AT VARIOUS LOCATIONS FEARING FOR MY SAFETY AND FEARING FOR THE SECURITY OF MY CAR.

I WAS GETTING WORRIED ABOUT MY RESPONSIBILITY TO JOHN REGAN, WHO I HAD JUST BOUGHT THE CAR FROM, AND HAD JUST GIVEN HIM THE FIRST PAYMENT, A $200 CHECK.

I WAS ALSO THINKING ABOUT MY FRIEND JEFF, EXPECTING ME UP NORTH IN DEER CREEK ON SATURDAY 8/8/87, WHO DIDN'T KNOW OF MY WHEREABOUTS.

IT WENT LIKE THIS...

INSTANT CASH — CRACK HOUSE — INSTANT CASH — CRACK HOUSE — INSTANT CASH

CRACK HOUSE — WHEW! BALANCE: $0.00 THANK-YOU / OUT OF CASH — CHECK CASHING COMPANY — THA'S OUR CHUMP HAR HAR

WHERE NEXT? HA HA HA
I CAN'T BELIEVE THIS IS HAPPENING...
CHECK CASHING COMPANY

CRACK HOUSE

CHECK CASHING COMPANY, CRACK HOUSE, DRUG STORE, GAS STATION, CRACK HOUSE, CHECK CASHING COMPANY, CRACK HOUSE, ETC.

Panel 1
FOR THE RECORD, THE CHECK REGISTER FROM THE VICTIMS CHECKING ACCOUNT WHICH CONTAINS ENTRIES TO VARIOUS CHECK CASHING COMPANIES, DRUG STORES, DEPARTMENT STORES, GAS STATIONS, AND VARIOUS INDIVIDUALS, HAS BEEN EXAMINED AND TAKEN AS EVIDENCE AND PROPERTY INVENTORIED BY SGT. STREAM.

Panel 2
Q: WERE ANY OTHER SPECIFIC THREATS MADE AND BY WHOM?
A: I WAS SPECIFICALLY THREATENED PRACTICALLY EVERYTIME WE STOPPED SOMEWHERE, TO INSURE MY COOPERATION.

Panel 3
Q: DID ALL THREE PARTIES MAKE THOSE THREATS?
A: YES, THEY WERE TRYING TO FIRE EACH OTHER UP BY THEIR STATEMENTS — IT WAS LIKE THEY WERE A GANG.

"WE NEED MORE **MONEY**!"

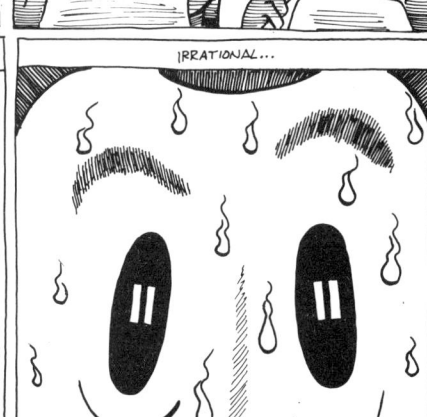

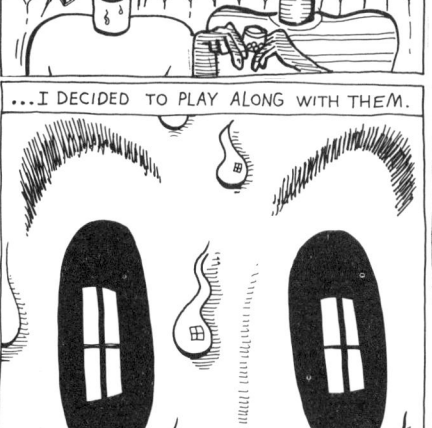

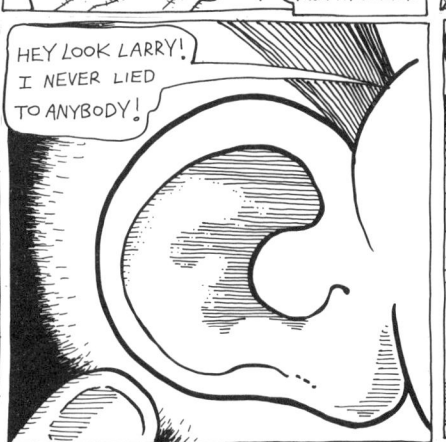

Panel 4
Q: CAN YOU DESCRIBE FOR ME HOW YOU WERE ABLE TO GET AWAY FROM THE SUSPECTS?
A: YES — BY SUNDAY AFTERNOON, AFTER 30 SOME HOURS OF THIS ABDUCTION THING...

Panel 5
...BY THAT TIME I WAS SO SCARED, DESPERATE,

Panel 6
IRRATIONAL...

Panel 7
...I DECIDED TO PLAY ALONG WITH THEM.

Panel 8
HA HA HA HA HA HA HA HA HA HA HA HA!!

HUH? WHA'S O FUNNY?

DESPERATE → WIRED →

NOW WEARING A SHIRT STOLEN FROM MY BACKPACK

Panel 9
"IT JUST DOESN'T MATTER ANYMORE! HA HA! I GIVE UP! I'VE WRITTEN A MILLION CHECKS AND I ONLY HAD $150! HA HA HA! I GUESS THAT MAKES ME A CRIMINAL TOO, HUH? HA HA HA HA"

PUNCH

Panel 10

Panel 11
HEY LOOK LARRY! I NEVER LIED TO ANYBODY!

Panel 12
HA HA HA HA HA HA HA HA HAR HAR HAR

HA HA HA, THAS FUNNY... I LIKE THAT HEE HEE
HAR! HE'S FOOTIN' THE BILL GIV'IM A HIT!
OH NO!
ASHED
HECKS
ASHED
OPEN
UH, SURE GUYS... I'LL TRY A.. HIT (GULP!)
NOW INHALE SLOWLY....
URGH... I FEEL SICK... LIKE I MIGHT..
HAR HAR! THAS WHEN YOU KNOW IT'S GOOD! WHEN IT MAKES YOU SICK LIKE PUKIN' ITS PURE!
GAG!
YAWN
AT 5:30 PM THEY LET ME DRIVE MY OWN CAR AND SEEMED TO TRUST ME TO DRIVE. "DEE" WAS IN THE PASSENGER SEAT. (THE OTHERS WERE BUYING CRACK)
AT THIS TIME "DEE" WAS TALKING TO A GUY BY THE NAME OF "MARK" WHO HAD WALKED UP TO THE CAR AND HE WAS TRYING TO SELL MARIJUANA AND GOT INTO THE BACKSEAT.
"DEE" TOLD MARK TO LIGHT A JOINT RIGHT AWAY BECAUSE I WAS REALLY NERVOUS AND HAD BEEN THROUGH A LOT OF HELL DURING THE LAST DAY.
HOW OLD ARE YOU, MARK?
17.
17?! WHAT ARE YOU DOING THIS FOR?
GOOD MONEY, DRUGS, MONEY
DRUGS HAR HAR
HE LIT A JOINT AND THEN "DEE" AND "MARK" GOT INTO AN ARGUMENT ABOUT PAYING FOR THE JOINT AND "DEE" TOLD "MARK" TO GET OUT OF THE CAR WHICH HE DID.
SHORTLY THEREAFTER "DEE" GOT OUT OF THE CAR FROM THE PASSENGERS SEAT AND STOOD BY THE CAR WITH ONE FOOT ON THE THRESHOLD OF THE PASSENGERS SIDE AND HIS ARMS ON TOP OF THE WINDOW AND ON TOP OF THE CAR WHILE HE WAS TALKING TO "MARK".

I SAW THAT THIS WAS MY OPPORTUNITY TO GET AWAY AND I HIT THE ACCELERATOR AND SPED OFF SOUTH ON PLEASANT TOWARDS LAKE.
WHEN I GOT TO LAKE STREET I NOTICED A CAR WITH TWO BLACK MALES BEHIND ME. IT COULD HAVE BEEN ANYONE, BUT BEING PARANIOD, I DROVE STRAIGHT DOWN LAKE STREET TO THE LAKES AND DROVE AROUND UNTIL I WAS SURE THAT I WASN'T BEING FOLLOWED AND DROVE TO MY FRIEND MIKE'S HOUSE, WHERE I CALLED THE POLICE.
BOB! BE CAREFUL THEY KNOW WHERE WE LIVE! I'M CALLING THE POLICE!
(ROOMMATE)
WHA?
WERE ANY HOMOSEXUAL OVERTURES MADE TO YOU BY THE SUSPECTS?
WHAT? NO!
WERE YOU ALLOWED TO SLEEP AT ANYTIME DURING THIS PERIOD OF TIME?
NO
DO YOU HAVE ANYTHING TO ADD OR SUBTRACT FROM THIS STATEMENT?
I WOULD LIKE TO READ IT FIRST
IS THIS STATEMENT GIVEN OF YOUR OWN FREE WILL AND ACCORD WITHOUT ANY THREATS OR PROMISES BEING MADE?
YES..
IF NECESSARY, WILL YOU ASSIST IN PROSECUTION?
...YES
AFTER GIVEN THE OPPORTUNITY TO READ YOUR STATEMENT AND FIND IT TO BE TRUE AND CORRECT, AS GIVEN, WILL YOU SIGN IT AS SUCH?
THANK YOU FOR THIS STATEMENT THIS IS THE THIRD TIME THESE GUYS HAVE BEEN IN HERE. MAYBE SOMETHING WILL STICK THIS TIME.
THIRD?!
NOW I UNDERSTAND THAT YOUR ROOMMATE, MR. ROBERT CARDOZA, WILL BE MAKING A STATEMENT TOMORROW AT 7:30 AM
DON'T WORRY, PAT THESE GUYS AREN'T DANGEROUS. I CALL THEM "POP CORN PIMPS"
YEA, I'LL REMIND'IM TONIGHT
HEH HEH
ANTIQUES WHOLESALE
SIGH
OPEN
Antiques Wholesale
7:30 AM
MOTORHEAD

7:30 AM

"HELLO, YOU MUST BE ROBERT CARDOZA THE CONSTITUTION REQUIRES THAT I INFORM YOU... BLA BLA... ANYTHING YOU SAY CAN BE USED... BLA... BLA BLA..."

TAP TAP TAP

"DO YOU UNDERSTAND THESE RIGHTS?"

"YES"

"ARE YOU FAMILIAR WITH THE VICTIM IN THIS CASE, PATRICK MORIARITY?"

"YES, HE'S MY ROOMMATE AND I HAVE KNOWN HIM APPROXIMATELY 6 MONTHS"

Q: CALLING YOUR ATTENTION TO SUNDAY 8-9-87, AT APPROXIMATELY 1700 HRS, DID YOU RECIEVE A PHONE CALL FROM PATRICK?
A: YES SIR I DID. I ARRIVED HOME AROUND 5 PM AND RIGHT WHEN I WALKED IN THE DOOR THE PHONE RANG AND I THOUGHT THEY HAD ASKED FOR BOB AND I SAID I WAS BOB AND THIS PARTY SOUNDED LIKE A BLACK GENTLEMEN WHO SAID HE WAS MARK, TALKING IN A REAL JIVE VOICE, ASKING ME "DO YOU REMEMBER ME AT 28TH AND YOU WOULDN'T GIVE ME A RIDE?"

"HUH?"

I THEN SAID THAT I DIDN'T KNOW HIM AND HE ASKED IF I WAS PAT AND I TOLD HIM THAT HE WASN'T HOME AND THAT WAS THE END OF OUR CONVERSATION.

(CLICK)

RIGHT AFTER THAT I RECIEVED A CALL AGAIN AND IT WAS PAT AND HE SOUNDED VERY DISTRESSED, HIS VOICE WAS QUIVERING AND HE SOUNDED LIKE HE WAS READY TO CRY. I ASKED HIM WHAT WAS WRONG SO HE GAVE ME A BRIEF SYNOPSIS OVER THE PHONE ABOUT HIS BEING HELD HOSTAGE FOR THE LAST DAY AND A HALF —

JEEZ!

HE SAID THAT 3 BLACK GUYS FORCED HIM TO DRIVE THEM AROUND TOWN, TOOK HIS CAR, AND FORCED HIM TO CASH OVER $600 IN CHECKS. SO HE TOLD ME HE WAS OVER AT MIKE CAMBELLS, AND THAT HE DIDN'T WANT TO COME HOME BECAUSE HE WAS AFRAID THAT THESE 3 BLACK GUYS WOULD COME OVER TO THE HOUSE AND THAT HE WAS JUST CALLING THE HOUSE TO WARN US THAT THEY MIGHT BE COMING.

I GOT OFF THE PHONE THEN AND LOOKED OUTSIDE AND THERE WERE THREE (3) BMs SITTING ACROSS THE STREET ON THE STEPS OF THE BUILDING, AND THEY SEEMED LIKE THEY WERE WATCHING OUR HOUSE, STARING UP AT THE HOUSE.

Antiques Wholesale

SO I CALLED MIKE CAMBELL'S HOUSE AND TALKED TO PAT AND TOLD HIM OF THESE 3 BMs THAT WERE SITTING OUT IN FRONT OF OUR HOUSE ACROSS THE STREET AND TOLD HIM TO COME HOME AND SEE IF THESE WERE THE SAME 3 GUYS SO THAT WE COULD CALL THE POLICE AND HAVE THEM ARRESTED.

IT WAS ABOUT THAT TIME THAT THEY LEFT. I WOULD LIKE TO ADD THAT PAT WAS SOMEWHAT HESITANT OF CALLING THE POLICE IN FEAR OF RETALIATION BUT I MANAGED TO CONVINCE HIM TO CALL THE POLICE AND REPORT IT FROM MIKE CAMBELL'S HOUSE.

Q: DID PATRICK SUBSEQUENTLY COME HOME?
A: YES, HE CAME HOME AND SAW TWO OF THE PARTIES I DESCRIBED TO HIM ON THE PHONE AND AT THIS TIME THEY WERE OVER AT THE CORNER AND HE SAID THAT THEY WERE NOT THE PARTIES THAT HAD ABDUCTED HIM.

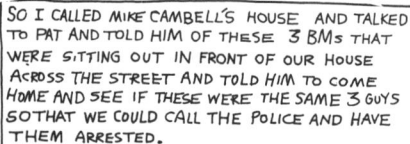

"NOPE"

Panel	Text
1	"WHAT CONVERSATION DID YOU HAVE WITH PATRICK UPON HIS ARRIVAL BACK HOME?" / "HE TOLD ME THE FULL STORY IN DETAIL THAT SATURDAY MORNING..."
2	"...THREATENED HIM WITH BODILY HARM IF HE FAILED TO COOPERATE IN CASHING CHECKS OR IF HE SCREWED UP IN ANY WAY BY TRYING TO ESCAPE — THAT THEY WOULD KICK HIS ASS, AND TAKE HIS CAR. WHEN I SAW HIM, HE WAS SHAKING AND REALLY DISTRESSED."
3	Q: DID YOU HAVE ANY SUBSEQUENT CONTACT WITH THE PARTIES THAT PATRICK HAD IDENTIFIED AS HIS KIDNAPPERS? A: AT 7AM, ON MONDAY MORNING, WE WERE AWAKENED BY SOMEONE CALLING FROM OUTSIDE THE HOUSE — ZZZ ZZZ Z...YO?
4	THEY WERE CALLING UP "YO, PAT, YO, PAT" / "HUH? OH GOD WILL THIS NIGHTMARE EVER END?"
5	I GOT DRESSED AND WENT DOWNSTAIRS AND PAT WAS IN THE HALLWAY TALKING WITH 2 BMs AND THEY WERE TRYING TO CONVINCE HIM THAT THEY HAD MONEY AND WANTED TO PAY HIM BACK, / ↑ BEING TOUGH BEHIND A LOCKED DOOR
6	SO WHEN I ARRIVED DOWNSTAIRS I APPROACHED THESE PARTIES AND OBSERVED THAT THEY WERE TRYING TO CONVINCE PAT TO GIVE THEM A RIDE AND GET THEM MORE MONEY AND I TOLD THEM TO GET OUT AS THEY HAD ALREADY RIPPED HIM OFF ONCE.
7	"YOU RIP THIS GUY OFF AND YOU'VE GOT THE NERVE TO COME BACK HERE? GET THE 9#☆k OUT OF HERE AND DON'T COME BACK!"
8	"RIP HIM AAWF?! RIP HIM AAWF?! MAN, WE'S TRYING TO HELP THE DUDE. WE GOT MONEY FOR HIM. WE JUS' NEED A RIDE..."
9	(sweating face)
10	"ALRIGHT! I'VE HAD IT! JUST LEAVE NOW!" / Antiques
11	WE HAD A BRIEF ARGUMENT AND THEY FINALLY LEFT AND WENT ACROSS THE STREET TO THE SAME FILLING STATION WHERE WE OBSERVED THEM TRYING TO STOP CARS AND GET INTO THEM. / "SCUSE ME..." "HI" "HUH?" / MARTIN LUTHER KING JR / GAS SELF-SERV / LIQUOR / "I DON'T BELIEVE IT! WOULDJA LOOK AT THAT!"
12	PAT CALLED 911, THE POLICE ARRIVED AND ARRESTED THESE TWO BLACK MALES. / "YES... SAME TWO GUYS I DESCRIBED LAST NIGHT... THEY'RE AT THE SAME STATION AGAIN... YES... CLOTHES? THEY'RE DRESSED THE SAME TOO, MUSTA BEEN WIRED ALL NIGHT AGAIN... THEY'RE HASSELIN PEOPLE IN THE LOT... HURRY BEFORE THEY GET A RIDE..!!"

GOT A CAR?
YO...UH OH
THERE THEY ARE
POLICE
PULL OVER
OVER HERE!
GAS
GRRRR
HEY! DON'T @☆#K WITH US!
LOOK YOU! KEEP LOOKING FOR REVENGE LIKE THAT AND YOU'RE OFF TO JAIL TOO! I KNOW ABOUT THIS HOUSE AND ALL THOSE WILD LOUD BEER PARTIES YOU THROW! NOW KNOCK IT OFF OR I'LL FIND A REASON TO TURN YOU IN TOO WISE GUY!
BOB, THIS IS MY BUSINESS. I APPRECIATE YOUR CONCERN BUT I REALLY DON'T WANT HASSLES WITH THE COPS TOO. PLEASE, JUST GO UPSTAIRS AND LET ME HANDLE THIS.
ALRIGHT ALREADY! GRUMBLE GRUMBLE
WHY, I OUTTA...
WE'LL TALK TO THE GUY... STAY CLOSE TO THE SUSPECTS
GAS
ANTIQUES
OPEN

IS THIS THE AUTO INVOLVED IN THE ABDUCTION?
YES
MAY WE USE THIS CAR TO DUST FOR FINGERPRINTS AND LOOK FOR EVIDENCE?
YES. ONE OF THOSE GUYS IS WEARING MY SHIRT. THE HAWAIIAN ONE IS HIS IN THE BACK.
WHAT HAPPENS NOW?
WE'LL SCHEDULE YOU TO MAKE A STATEMENT WITH SGT. STREAM.
WHAT ABOUT THESE GUYS?
DON'T WORRY. I BELIEVE THEY'LL BE PUT AWAY FOR QUITE AWHILE.
AFTER THE COPS ARE GONE...
WAIT! WHERE ARE YOU GOING WITH MY CAR?!
IMPOUND LOT
TOWIN
BY FRED + C
THE IMPOUND LOT! WHY?
POLICE ORDER. I DON'T KNOW OR CARE WHY. IT'LL COST'YA 50 BUCKS TO GET IT BACK FROM THE LOT.
BUT I HAVEN'T BROKEN ANY LAWS! I GAVE THE POLICE PERMISSION TO DUST MY CAR FOR EVIDENCE!
TAKE IT UP WITH THE POLICE BUB
MAN! WHAT A WEEKEND FROM HELL... BETTER FIGURE A WAY TO WORK THIS MORNING... THEN I GOTTA W....
I AM SHOWING YOU A PHOTO LINE-UP OF EIGHT (8) YOUNG ADULT BMs — — DO YOU RECOGNIZE ANY OF THEM?
PHOTO #4 & PHOTO #7 ARE THE TWO PARTIES I OBSERVED AT MY HOUSE ON MONDAY MORNING, 8/10/87
FOR THE RECORD, THE WITNESS HAS IDENTIFIED PHOTO #4 WHICH IS THAT OF LEXY SMITH, AND PHOTO #7 WHICH SHOWS THE NAME ON THE PHOTO AS DARREN SMITH. THESE PHOTOS HAVE BEEN SIGNED BY THE WITNESS.
10
4
12
7
8
2
3
9
TAP
TAP
TAP
TAP
IS THERE ANYTHING THAT YOU WISH TO ADD OR SUBTRACT FROM YOUR STATEMENT?
: I JUST WANT TO GET ACROSS HOW I THINK THIS CRIME IS SERIOUS AND THE FACT THAT I BELIEVE 100% PAT'S STORY, DETAIL TO DETAIL, BECAUSE HE IS JUST NOT THE TYPE OF PERSON WHO COULD EVER HURT ANYBODY OR EXAGGERATE A STORY LIKE THIS — HE IS THE TYPE OF PERSON WHO CANNOT LIE OR KNOW HOW TO LIE AND DOESN'T HAVE A MALICIOUS BONE IN HIS BODY. I AM SAYING THIS BECAUSE I WANT TO SEE THIS CASE PROSECUTED TO THE FULL EXTENT OF THE LAW BECAUSE I KNOW HOW BADLY THIS HAS SHAKEN PAT UP AND IT WILL HAVE A VERY LONG LASTING EFFECT ON HIM.
IS THIS STATEMENT GIVEN OF YOUR OWN FREE WILL WITHOUT ANY THREATS OR PROMISES BEING MADE?
YES
IF NECESSARY, WILL YOU ASSIST IN PROSECUTION?
YES
AFTER READING THIS STATEMENT AND FINDING IT TO BE TRUE + CORRECT, WOULD YOU BE WILLING TO SIGN IT?
YES

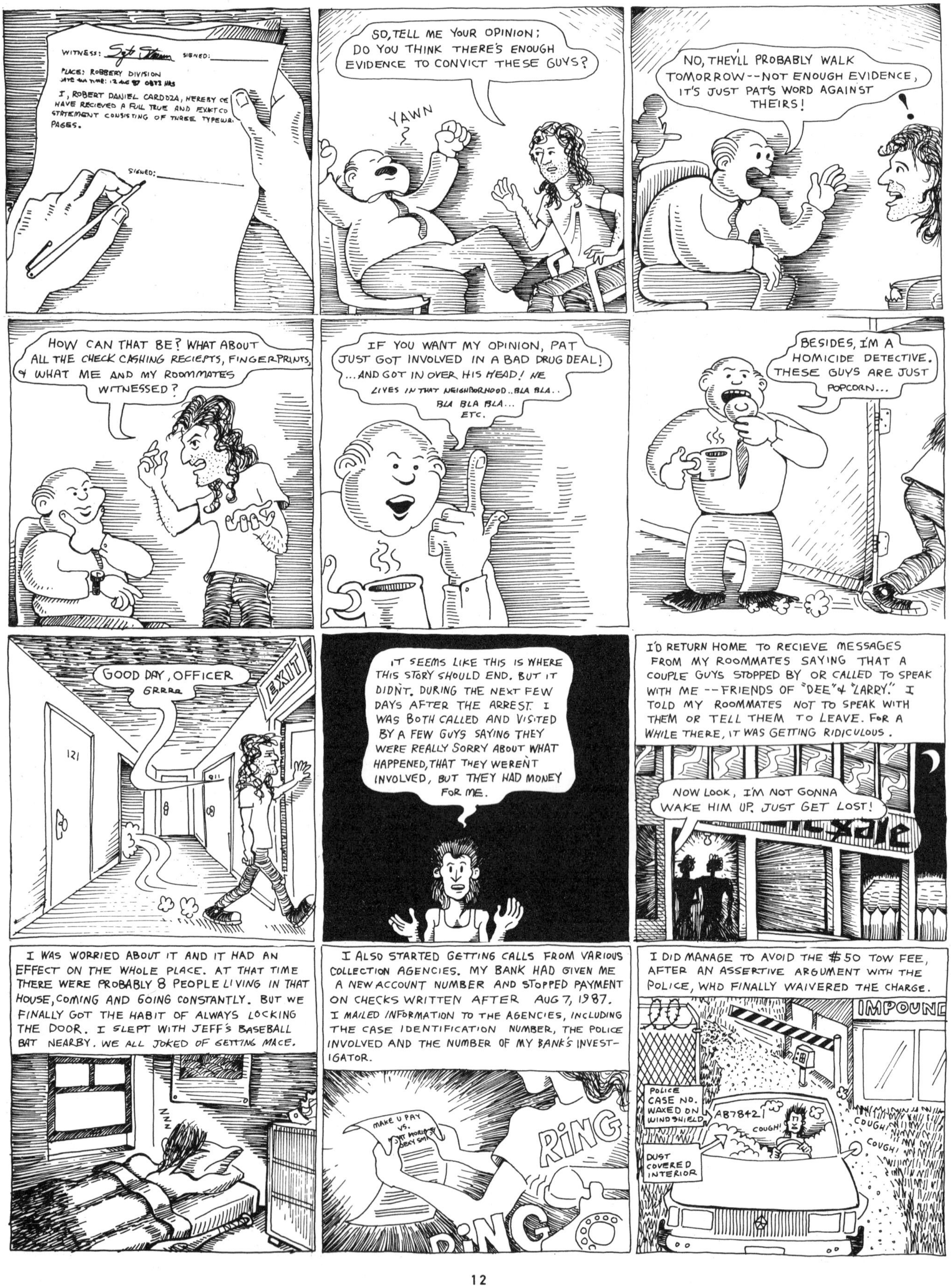

WITNESS: Sgt Stearn SIGNED:
PLACE: ROBBERY DIVISION
DATE AND TIME: 12 AUG 87 0873 HRS
I, ROBERT DANIEL CARDOZA, HEREBY CE
HAVE RECIEVED A FULL TRUE AND EXACT CO
STATEMENT CONSISTING OF THREE TYPEWR
PAGES.
SIGNED:
SO, TELL ME YOUR OPINION; DO YOU THINK THERE'S ENOUGH EVIDENCE TO CONVICT THESE GUYS?
YAWN
NO, THEY'LL PROBABLY WALK TOMORROW--NOT ENOUGH EVIDENCE, IT'S JUST PAT'S WORD AGAINST THEIRS!
!
HOW CAN THAT BE? WHAT ABOUT ALL THE CHECK CASHING RECIEPTS, FINGERPRINTS, & WHAT ME AND MY ROOMMATES WITNESSED?
IF YOU WANT MY OPINION, PAT JUST GOT INVOLVED IN A BAD DRUG DEAL! ...AND GOT IN OVER HIS HEAD! HE LIVES IN THAT NEIGHBORHOOD.. BLA BLA.. BLA BLA BLA... ETC.
BESIDES, I'M A HOMICIDE DETECTIVE. THESE GUYS ARE JUST POPCORN...
GOOD DAY, OFFICER GRRRR
EXIT
121
IT SEEMS LIKE THIS IS WHERE THIS STORY SHOULD END. BUT IT DIDN'T. DURING THE NEXT FEW DAYS AFTER THE ARREST I WAS BOTH CALLED AND VISITED BY A FEW GUYS SAYING THEY WERE REALLY SORRY ABOUT WHAT HAPPENED, THAT THEY WEREN'T INVOLVED, BUT THEY HAD MONEY FOR ME.
I'D RETURN HOME TO RECIEVE MESSAGES FROM MY ROOMMATES SAYING THAT A COUPLE GUYS STOPPED BY OR CALLED TO SPEAK WITH ME --FRIENDS OF "DEE" & "LARRY." I TOLD MY ROOMMATES NOT TO SPEAK WITH THEM OR TELL THEM TO LEAVE. FOR A WHILE THERE, IT WAS GETTING RIDICULOUS.
NOW LOOK, I'M NOT GONNA WAKE HIM UP, JUST GET LOST!
I WAS WORRIED ABOUT IT AND IT HAD AN EFFECT ON THE WHOLE PLACE. AT THAT TIME THERE WERE PROBABLY 8 PEOPLE LIVING IN THAT HOUSE, COMING AND GOING CONSTANTLY. BUT WE FINALLY GOT THE HABIT OF ALWAYS LOCKING THE DOOR. I SLEPT WITH JEFF'S BASEBALL BAT NEARBY. WE ALL JOKED OF GETTING MACE.
ZZZ
I ALSO STARTED GETTING CALLS FROM VARIOUS COLLECTION AGENCIES. MY BANK HAD GIVEN ME A NEW ACCOUNT NUMBER AND STOPPED PAYMENT ON CHECKS WRITTEN AFTER AUG 7, 1987. I MAILED INFORMATION TO THE AGENCIES, INCLUDING THE CASE IDENTIFICATION NUMBER, THE POLICE INVOLVED AND THE NUMBER OF MY BANK'S INVESTIGATOR.
MAKE U PAY VS.
RING
RING
I DID MANAGE TO AVOID THE $50 TOW FEE, AFTER AN ASSERTIVE ARGUMENT WITH THE POLICE, WHO FINALLY WAIVERED THE CHARGE.
IMPOUND
POLICE CASE NO. WAXED ON WINDSHIELD
AB7842
COUGH!
COUGH!
COUGH!
DUST COVERED INTERIOR

ALL IN ALL, MY BANK WAS PRETTY GOOD ABOUT THE WHOLE THING, SURPRIZINGLY. I STAYED WITH THEM ALTHOUGH I WAS TO PAY A $50 "FEE" FOR CHANGING ACCOUNT NUMBERS.
SGT. STREAM CALLED ME A FEW DAYS AFTER THE ARREST...
YOU WON'T BE HARASSED ANYMORE. WE RELEASED THEM YESTERDAY.
WHAT?! WHY DIDN'T YOU TELL ME? THEY KNOW WHERE I LIVE!
THEY'LL TRY SOMEONE ELSE THIS TIME. MAYBE WE'LL GET THEM IF WE CAN COMPILE ENOUGH OF THESE INCIDENTS TOGETHER TO FORM A STRONGER CASE.
THATS WHEN I LEARNED ABOUT THE STATE'S 36 HOUR RULE. IT'S THE LEGAL REQUIREMENT THAT SUSPECTS MUST BE CHARGED FORMALLY OR BE RELEASED WITHIN 36 HOURS OF THEIR ARREST.
THERE WAS REALLY NO CASE IN DRUG POSSESSION — THERE WERE NO DRUGS TO BE FOUND, ALTHOUGH THERE MAY HAVE BEEN A GLASS TUBE STUFFED WITH SCRATCH PAD CHUNKS SOMEWHERE IN THE CAR... AND THERE'S ALSO THE LAW ON "CONSTRUCTIVE POSSESSION", ANYWAY. THAT'S THE LEGAL REQUIREMENT THAT IN ORDER TO PROSECUTE SOMEONE FOR DRUG POSSESSION, YOU MUST PROVE THAT THE PERSON SOMEHOW HAS CONTROL OF THE DRUGS ALLEGEDLY IN HIS OR HER POSSESSION, EVEN IF THE DRUGS ARE LYING RIGHT THERE WHEN THE POLICE ARRIVE.
I SAID THEY HAD DRUGS, AND THEY PROBABLY DENIED IT, I SAID I WAS ABDUCTED, OR HIJACKED, KIDNAPPED OR WHATEVER, AND THEY PROBABLY DENIED IT. THE COPS HAVE 36 HOURS TO PULL TOGETHER THE EVIDENCE THAT WILL PROVE BEYOND A REASONABLE DOUBT THAT THE CRIME WAS COMMITTED BY THE DEFENDANTS, WHO WILL SURELY DENY IT. SO FAR, THESE TWO GUYS HAD BEEN ARRESTED AND RELEASED 3 OR 4 TIMES ALREADY. FOR THE SAME THINGS!
HOW MANY TIMES DO THESE GUYS HAVE TO GET ARRESTED BEFORE IT CONSTITUTES SOMETHING SERIOUS?
THERE WASN'T ENOUGH EVIDENCE FOR ANYTHING IN MY CASE. IT DOESN'T MATTER MUCH, BUT LARRY STILL HAS MY SHIRT... WHEN I GOT MY CAR BACK I FOUND HIS HAWIIAN SHIRT STILL INSIDE, OVERLOOKED OR IGNORED BY THE POLICE.
I KEPT IN GOOD CONTACT WITH SGT. STREAM AND HEARD A FEW DETAILS TO SEVERAL ADDITIONAL ARRESTS OF THE SMITH BROTHERS.
STREAM EVENTUALLY SAID THAT THE SMITHS WERE GETTING COCKY ABOUT THEIR ARRESTS, KNOWING THAT THEY'D BE RELEASED IN 36 HOURS

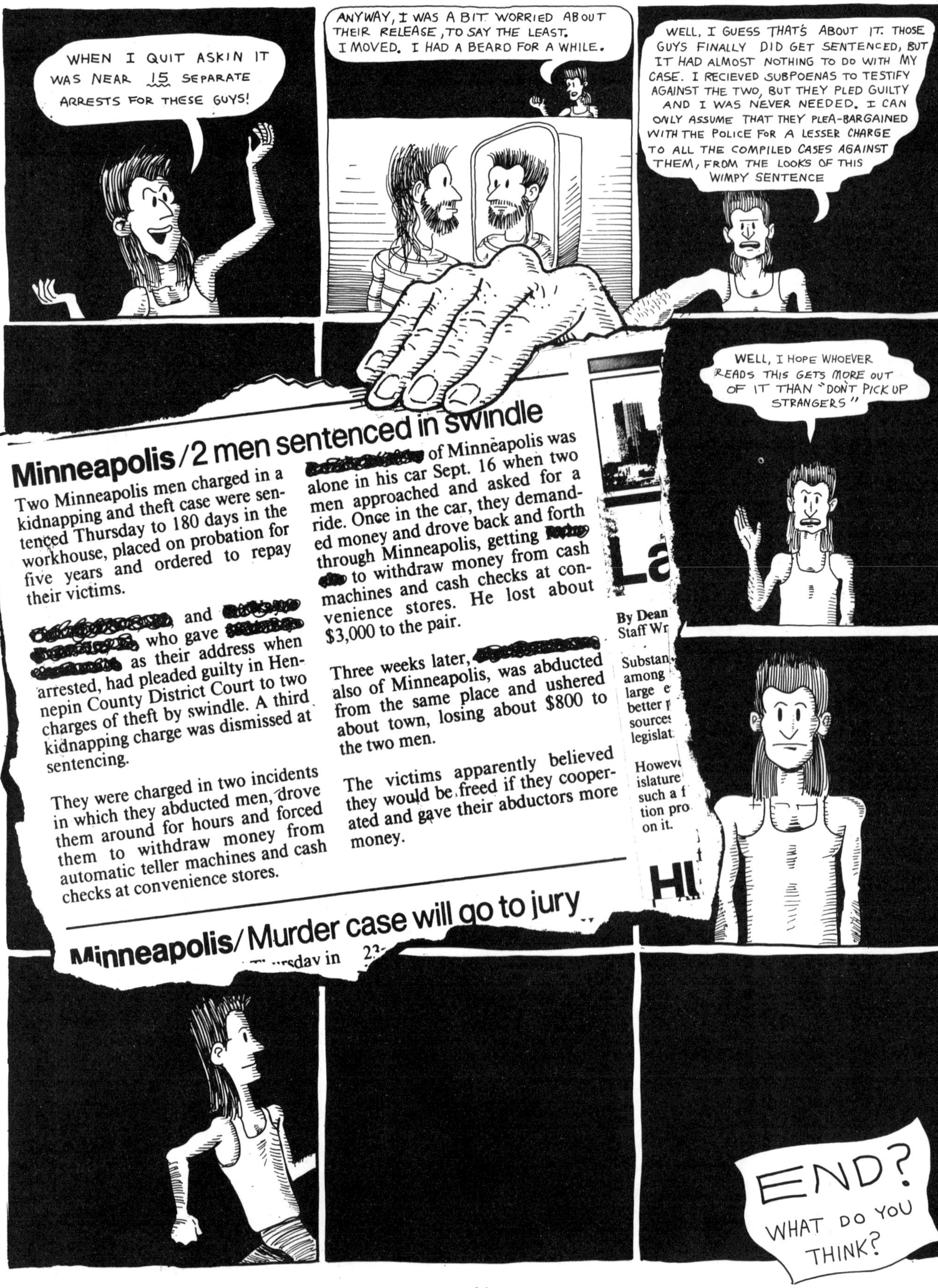

AND NOW... A BIT ON NAUGHTY BITS

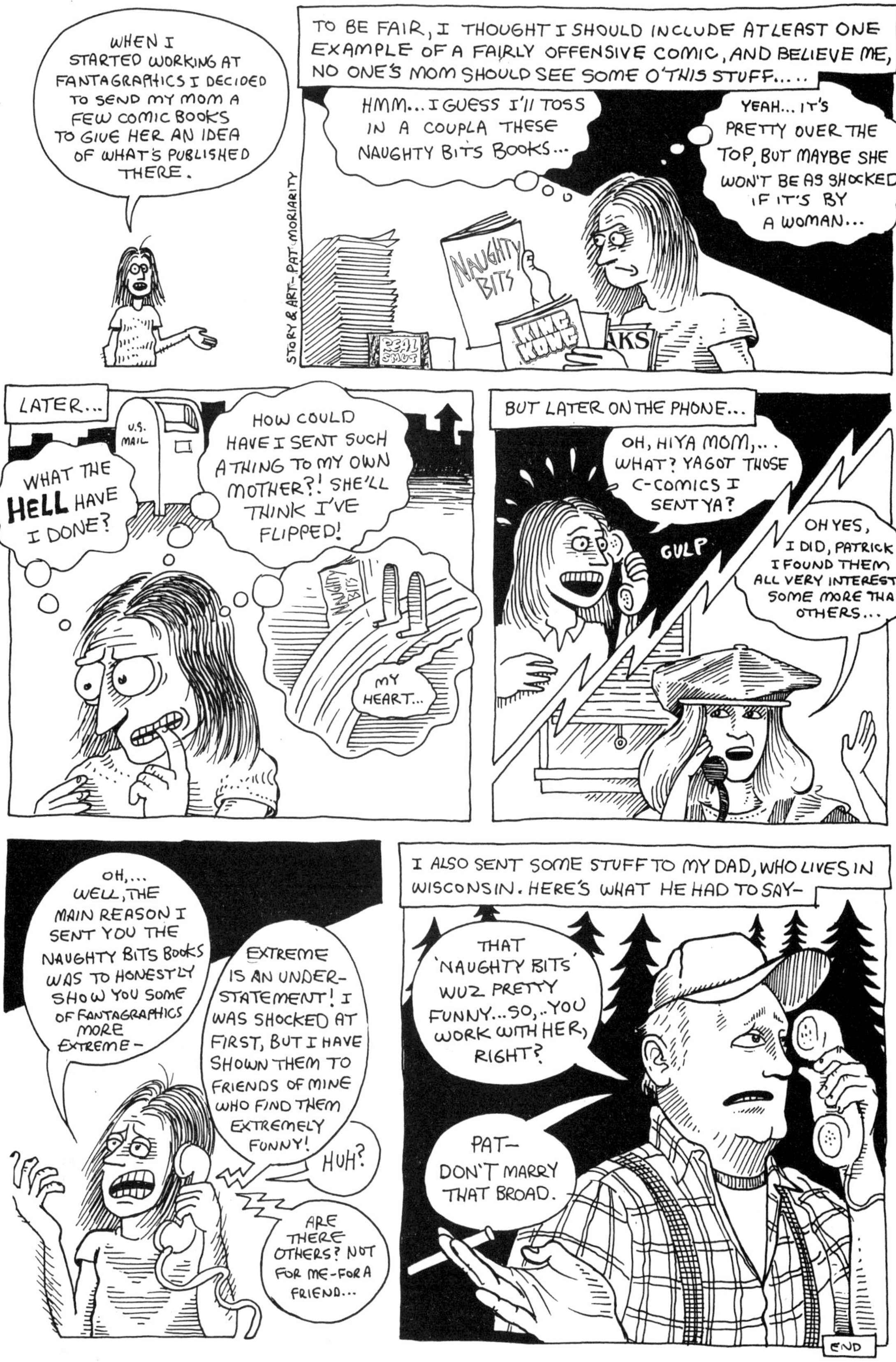

DEATH OF A JUNKIE

STORY BY DENNIS P. EICHHORN • CARTOONS BY PAT MORIARITY

IT WAS SPRINGTIME IN SEATTLE, AND I WAS A NEWCOMER. ONE AFTERNOON I FOUND MYSELF AT THE SEATTLE CENTER, TAKING IN THE SIGHTS.

I WAS STANDING AT THE BASE OF THE SPACE NEEDLE, WHEN I SPOTTED A FAMILIAR FACE. IT WAS TIM GAZAWAY, A CASUAL ACQUAINTANCE FROM MY HOMETOWN OF BOISE, IDAHO.

HEY TIM! REMEMBER ME?

OH, YEAH... DENNY RIGHT? HOW ARE YOU DOIN'?

WHAT'S WITH THE COVERALLS, TIM?

I WORK HERE AT THE CENTER. THEY MAKE US WEAR THESE... LISTEN, I'M ALMOST DONE FOR THE DAY. MEET ME BY THE FOUNTAIN IN HALF AN HOUR AND WE'LL HAVE A CHANCE TO TALK.

OKAY

LATER

SO, UH, YOU EVER SMOKE POT, DENNY?

SURE

WELL, COME ON OVER TO MY PLACE

NEARLY EVERYONE IN THE BUILDING IS FROM IDAHO

THAT'S COOL.

IDAHO

?

THIS IS DENNY EICHHORN

AND THESE ARE MITCH, JACK AND RYAN.

I WENT TO BOISE HIGH

SO DID I

I'M FROM POCATELLO

NICE TO MEET YOU. I WENT TO BORAH HIGH

NICE
IF YOU WANT TO SCORE A LID WE'RE HOLDING
HOW MUCH?
FIFTEEN
HOW MUCH FOR FOUR?
FIFTY
LET ME THINK ABOUT IT FOR A FEW MINUTES
NOD
TIMO
WHERE'S YOUR BATHROOM?
THROUGH THERE

PEE-YOU
SNIFF
FLUSH
ODOR OF SHIT
?
ZIP
PUNGENT ODOR OF SHIT
FUCK THIS GUY'S DEAD!
MR CLEAN
LISTEN, THERE'S A GUY ON THE BED HERE WHO DOESN'T LOOK SO GOOD
!
!
MITCH JACK, TIM... SQUIRREL IS KAKKED!

BARF
GAG
ITS SO GROSS
HM
POKE
JESUS CHRIST SQUIRREL WAS JONESIN' REAL BAD, AND HE KEPT BUGGING ME FOR MORE SKAG
FINALLY, I TOLD HIM, 'FIRE UP SOME MR. CLEAN. IT'LL TAKE THE EDGE OFF.'
AND THAT'S EXACTLY WHAT THE DUMBFUCK DID!
LOOK! SQUIRREL EVEN FLAGGED THE MR. CLEAN
BLOOD & MR CLEAN
HERE!
$50
WHAT ARE YOU GONNA DO ABOUT HIM?
WE'LL TAKE CARE OF IT. YOUR NAME WON'T BE MENTIONED
GREAT! SEE YOU AROUND!
WHOOOSHH
AS THE DAYS PAST, I READ THE NEWSPAPERS LOOKING FOR SOME MENTION OF SQUIRREL'S DEATH. THERE WAS NOTHING. WEEKS, THEN MONTHS PASSED BY.
The Seattle Times
ONE DAY IN THE FALL I WENT TO THE SEATTLE CENTER. AS I WALKED ALONG THE PATH, I SPOTTED TIM, RAKING LEAVES.
HEY TIM, HOW'S IT GOING? STILL LIVING IN THE SAME PLACE?
YOU BET. COME ON BY ANYTIME.

WHAT EVER HAPPENED TO THAT DEAD GUY?...YOU KNOW, SQUIRREL?
NOTHING. YOU KNOW, SQUIRREL WAS KIND OF A MYSTERY TO US.
HE WAS LIVING IN THE BUILDING WHEN I MOVED IN...
...DEALING DOPE AND SHOOTING UP EVERYTHING THAT CAME ALONG!
WHAT WAS HIS REAL NAME?
NOBODY KNOWS FOR SURE. HE WAS FROM BACK EAST SOMEPLACE. WE DIDN'T KNOW WHO TO CALL ABOUT HIM...
AND NOBODY WAS ANXIOUS TO BRING THE COPS AROUND
SO WHAT DID YOU DO?
WE JUST WAITED UNTIL DARK.
WE ROLLED HIM UP IN THE BEDDING AND CARRIED HIM OUT THE BACK WAY TO RYAN'S VW VAN.
3426
THEN JACK AND RYAN DROVE OUT IN THE COUNTRY AND DUMPED HIM IN A RAVINE OUT NEAR WOODINVILLE.
AS FAR AS WE KNOW, NOBODY'S FOUND HIM YET.
AND THAT WAS THE END OF IT.

MY LIFE IS GETTING TOO PREDICTABLE

THE MAN WITH 2 MISTRESSES!!
THAT'S ME.
HEH HEH
ONCE UPON A TIME, A MAN WITH SALT & PEPPER HAIR HAD TWO MISTRESSES, ONE YOUNG AND ONE NOT-SO-YOUNG. NEITHER MISTRESS KNEW ABOUT THE OTHER, AND NEITHER MISTRESS HAD LET HIM SO MUCH AS KISS HER--YET. LET'S JOIN HIM IN THE APARTMENT OF THE NOT-SO- … TRESS.
YOU'RE THE FAIREST CREATURE IN ALL THE WORLD!
YOU ARE THE ONLY WOMAN FOR ME!
KISS ME MY LOVE!
TUG
NOT TONIGHT
PARTING IS SUCH SWEET SORROW...
...I'LL BE BACK SOON, BABE!
PERHAPS THEN WE'LL KISS?
PERHAPS
12
ACROSS TOWN
YOU ARE THE FAIREST CREATURE IN ALL THE WORLD!
YOU'RE THE ONLY WOMAN FOR ME...
KISS ME, MY LOVE!
NOT TONIGHT

OH, BUT PARTING IS SUCH SWEET SORROW!
...I'LL BE BACK SOON!
PERHAPS THEN WE'LL KISS?
PERHAPS!
WHAT'S THIS?
OH NO!
THAT SCOUNDREL...
NOT SO YOUNG MISTRESS 25 MAIN ST. APT #2 555-2563 XXX000
THE YOUNG MISTRESS CALLED THE NOT SO YOUNG MISTRESS, AND TOGETHER THEY PLOTTED THEIR REVENGE...
LATER...
YOU WANT ME TO DO WHAT FOR A KISS?
IT'S SIMPLE, JUST LET ME PULL OUT YOUR GRAY HAIRS!
ATTENTION, NIT PICKERS! THE MAN NEVER NOTICED THAT THE NOTE WAS MISSING BECAUSE HE HAD MEMORIZED THE ADDRESS AND PHONE NUMBER OF THE NOT-SO-YOUNG MISTRESS AND ASSUMED HE'D THROWN OUT THE NOTE!
IF YOU HAD JUST YOUR BEAUTIFUL BLACK HAIR, YOU'D LOOK YOUNGER, WE'D BE A BETTER PHYSICAL MATCH, AND I'D FEEL SO MUCH MORE COMFORTABLE ABOUT KISSING YOU!
WELL, I GUESS IT'S ALRIGHT...

OUCH
ALMOST FINISHED
OUCH
OUCH
OUCH
OUCH
OUCH
I'M READY FOR MY KISS!
I'LL COME OVER TO YOUR APARTMENT AT 8 O'CLOCK TONIGHT TO GIVE YOU YOUR KISS!
I'LL BE WAITING, BABE.
12
ACROSS TOWN
KNOCK KNOCK
WHAT HAPPENED TO YOUR HAIR?!
UH...WELL,... I THOUGHT YOU'D KISS ME IF I LOOKED YOUNGER...
WELL,... YOU'RE WRONG!
BUT... IF YOU LET ME PULL OUT THE REST OF YOUR HAIR, YOU'LL LOOK OLDER, WE'LL MAKE A BETTER MATCH, AND I'LL FEEL MUCH MORE COMFORTABLE ABOUT KISSING YOU
WELL, I GUESS IT'S ALRIGHT...

NEARLY FINISHED!
OUCH
OUCH
OUCH
OUCH
OUCH
OUCH
OUCH
I'M READY FOR MY KISS!
I'LL COME OVER TO YOUR APARTMENT AT 10 O'CLOCK TONIGHT TO GIVE YOU YOUR KISS!
I'LL BE WAITING BABE!
HE STILL HASN'T CAUGHT ON, FOLKS!
8 O'CLOCK THAT EVENING...
AH! MY FIRST KISS
KNOCK
KNOCK
HUH?
POW
POW
OOOOF
BYE BYE BALDY!
PAT MORIARITY 91
WINK
HEH HEH, LOVE THEM WIMMEN!
END

TRUE STORY
SEPT 1990 IN WISC.
THAT CLOUD LOOKS LIKE A BIG GORILLA!
HEY, LOOK, THERE'S A GIANT CHICKEN!
?!
HEY, THIS PLACE MAKES FIBERGLASS FIGURES! LIKE THE BIG FAT HAPPY CHEF! PULL OVER!
WOW, CHECKOUT THESE MOLDS! AND FIGURES!
POOR COW
NO HEAD!
AND THIS MOUSE HAS NO HANDS.
MAN, IT'S LIKE A JUNKYARD OF ALL THIS COOL STUFF!
CHECK THIS OUT
STORY & ART BY PAT MORIARTY 1991
ITS THE A&W ROOT BEAR!
AND JESUS!
AND PARTS OF THE STATUE OF LIBERTY
HEY WATCH THIS!
GRUNT
WEIRD!
END

OREGON CHAIN-SAW MASSACRE
STORY BY MIKE CAMPBELL, MIKE LANG
ART BY PAT MORIARITY ©1991
I KNOW THIS GREAT TRAIL FOR HIKING, WHERE THE TREES ARE HUGE!
COOL. WHERE?
SAVE THE TREES
MT. HOOD!
HOW FAR IS IT!?
ABOUT 3 CUPS 'O JOE!
LET ME SEE THE MAP!
MT. HOOD NATIONAL FOREST
GREAT, THE NATIONAL FOREST!
OR NATIONAL CLEARCUT!
HUH?!
YEAH! IT'S A PUBLICLY OWNED FOREST. BUT THE BIG TIMBER COMPANIES ARE TURNING IT INTO A TREE FARM!
I THOUGHT THAT "NATIONAL FOREST" MEANT "PROTECTED"
NOPE.. LOOK AT THOSE CLEARCUTS!
HEY, THERE'S SOME REDNECK TAILGATING US!
HE'S RIGHT ON MY ASS!!
SLURP GLUG
SAVE THE TREES

TREE HUGGIN' SCUM!!
WHOOOAAA!
CRASH
WOW! CLOSE CALL!
WHAT WAS HIS PROBLEM?
I ♥ FRIED
KNUCKLE DRAGGING LOGGER!
LATER
GOD, LOOK HOW BIG THE TREES ARE!
FINALLY, THE OLD GROWTH FOREST!
EVERYTHING IS SO MAGESTIC
ONE THOUSAND YEARS TO GROW AND NINETY SECONDS TO FALL
WATCH IT! GET OUT OF HIS WAY!
AAIEEE!
SPIT
THAT WAS CLOSE!
THOSE LOG TRUCKERS GET PAID BY THE LOAD. THEY DRIVE LIKE THEY OWN THIS ROAD.
YOU COULD GET KILLED!
I CAN'T WAIT TO GET OUT OF THE CAR! BESIDES, THIS TRAIL I KNOW IS ABSOLUTELY GREAT!
YEAH, I BET HIKING AROUND HERE IS VISUALLY STIMULATING
RACE YA UP THAT HILL!
IT'S ALL... GONE!
END

ME SO HORNY

SITTIN' AT HOME WITH MY DICK ON HARD, I GOT THE BLACK BOOK FOR A FREAK TO CALL...

FLIP FLIP

FULL METAL JACKET

PICKED UP THE TELEPHONE, THEN DIALED THE SEVEN DIGITS, SAID:

YO, THIS MARQUIS, BABY ARE YOU DOWN WITH IT?

I ARRIVED AT HER HOUSE, KNOCKED ON THE DOOR, NOT HAVIN' NO IDEA WHAT THE NIGHT HAD IN STORE

KNOCK KNOCK

I'M LIKE A DOG IN HEAT, A FREAK WITHOUT WARNING, I HAVE AN APPETITE FOR SEX, BECAUSE ME SO HORNY

GIRLS ALWAYS ASK ME WHY I FUCK SO MUCH

WHAT'S WRONG, BABY DOLL, WITH A QUICK NUT?

'CAUSE YOU'RE THE ONE, AND YOU SHOULDN'T BE MAD

I WON'T TELL YOUR MOMMA IF YOU DON'T TELL YOUR DAD.

GRUNT

I KNOW HE'LL BE DISGUSTED WHEN HE SEES YOUR PUSSY'S BUSTED, WOULD YO' MOMMA BE SO MAD IF SHE KNEW I GOT THAT ASS!

HEE HEE

YOU CAN SAY I'M DESPERATE, YOU CAN CALL ME PERVERTED, BUT, YOU'LL SAY I'M A DOG, WHEN I LEAVE YOU FUCKIN' DESERTED!
JOB DONE
Z
I'LL PLAY WITH YOUR HEART — LIKE IT'S A GAME. I'LL BE BLOWIN' YOUR MIND WHILE YOU'RE BLOWIN' MY BRAIN
I'M JUS' LIKE THE MAN THEY CALL "GEORGIE PUDDIN' PIE", I FUCK ALL THE GIRLS AND I MAKE'M CRY.
AAUUGH
YOU'RE THE ONLY ONE, BABY
HMMF
GRUNT
I'M LIKE A DOG IN HEAT, A FREAK WITHOUT WARNING I HAVE AN APPETITE FOR SEX, 'CAUSE ME SO HORNY...
IT'S TRUE YOU WERE A VIRGIN, UNTIL YOU MET ME, I WAS THE FIRST TO MAKE YOU HOT AND WETTY WETTY
GEL
YOU TELL YOUR PARENTS THAT WE'RE GOIN' OUT
OVER 18
NEVER TO THE MOVIES, JUST STRAIGHT TO MY HOUSE.
GRUNT
ZIP
SLAM
SOCK IT TO ME
YOU SAID IT YOURSELF, YOU LIKE IT THAT WAY TOO, SO PUT YOUR LIPS ON MY DICK, AND SUCK MY ASSHOLE TOO, 'CAUSE I'M A FREAK IN HEAT, A DOG WITHOUT WARNING, I HAVE AN APPETITE FOR SEX, BECAUSE...
P. MORIARITY 91
ME SO HORNY!

A LOVE FANTASY
WORDS BY W. JOE
ART BY PAT M.
WELL, I PULL UP OUTSIDE HER HOUSE IN MY SKY ELECTRIC BLUE '53 ELDORADO CONVERTIBLE WITH THE WIRE WHEELS.
JUST LIKE IT SAYS THERE. IF YOU USE A PERSON'S HEAD, MAYBE JUST USE A SILHOUETTE. ADDS SOME MYSTERY DONCHA KNOW.
AND SHE'S OUT THE DOOR AND ONTO THE RED LEATHER SEAT BEFORE I CAN EVEN HONK THAT HORN ONCE.
FOR THIS, DRAW A CLOSE UP OF A PAIR OF SKIRTED THIGHS SITTING DOWN ON A TUCK AND ROLLED CAR SEAT!
SHE'S A VISION IN HER COWBOY BOOTS BIG BROWN EYES AND A WIDE RED MOUTH JUST LIKE PATSY CLINE'S
WHATEVER WORKS
WE POINT THAT CADDY WEST INTO THE SUNSET.
SHE PULLS A FIFTH OF JOSE CUERVO GOLD OUT OF HER RHINESTONE HANDBAG.
Tequila
Cuervo Especial
AND I BALANCE MY HANDS BETWEEN HER, THE BOTTLE AND THE STEERING WHEEL OUT INTO THE OPEN PRAIRIE. WITH THE SUN GOING DOWN.
OUT IN NEBRASKA THE BIG ORANGE MOON COMES UP AND SOME HEARTLAND RADIO IS PLAYING ALL OF OUR FAVORITE SONGS.
AND I'LL WALTZ ACROSS TEXAS WITH YOU DARLING...
IN THE DARK ON I-80 SHE PULLS HER REVOLVER OUT OF HER PURSE AND STARTS PICKING OFF THE LIGHTS OF THE BILLBOARDS.
BANG
BURM
SHAVE
I EMPTY THE BOTTLE OF TEQUILA, THROW IT UP, AND SHE SHOOTS IT INTO DIAMONDS OF SHATTERED GLASS. I'M WATCHING IT BURST IN THE REARVIEW MIRROR. WE START WORKING ON THE BOTTLE IN THE GLOVE COMPARTMENT.
BURP
CRASH
©1988 HOPPE/MORIARITY

Panel	Text
1	WE RIDE AND WE RIDE AND WE RIDE AND WE TELL EACH-OTHER EVERYTHING AND THE MILES SLIP BY UNDER THAT CADDY DOIN' UP EIGHTY AND THE RADIO STILL PULLS IN ALL OUR FAVORITE SONGS. "REALLY? YOU DON'T SAY..." BLA BLA
2	AND THE DISTANCES MELT AND I MELT AND SHE MELTS AND WE MELT INTO EACHOTHER DEEP INSIDE AND WE OPEN UP AND KNOW AND FEEL AND WE KNOW EACHOTHER AND WE KNOW THE ROAD AND WE KNOW AMERICA.
3	AND COME SUN UP COME DAWN WE HAVE ROLLED ALL THE WAY INTO LAS VEGAS, JEWEL OF THE DESERT. NEON LIT UP SEE IT FOR MILES. AND SMELL IT FOR AT LEAST THAT FAR.
4	AND WE PULL INTO THE GRACELAND WEDDING CHAPEL; TO GET MARRIED UNDER NEVADA LAW, SAYING THOSE VOWS AT DAWN.
5	TO STAGGER ACROSS THE STREET TO THE BLUE ROSEBUD TATOO EMPORIUM FOR MATCHING TATTOOS; HERS AND MINE. "RIGHT HERE PLEASE (HIC!)"
6	AWW YEAH BABY; ROSES AND DAGGERS AND A HEART WITH A BANNER ACROSS IT— "SWEETHEART—YOUR NAME HERE." —END— "AWW YEAH"
7	SEE PAT, THE THING IS THAT IT'S A FANTASY, RIGHT? SO MAYBE, OR MORE THAN LIKELY, THIS FANTASY WOMAN DOESN'T EXIST. THE LAST LINES AND FRAMES KIND OF EMPHASIZE THAT, I THINK.
8	SPEAKING OF FRAMES, I UNDERSTAND HOW THESE THINGS HAVE TO FIT ON THE PAGES. IF YOU NEED MORE OR LESS, DO WHAT YOU HAVE TO DO—AND THANKS ALOT. I WOULD REALLY LIKE TO SEE MY STUFF GET ILLUSTRATIONS. THEN IT WOULD BECOME ILLUSTRIOUS. HAR HAR HAR... END

34

AND A **DEAD DOG!**

AND A CUP OF PUS FROM GRANDMA'S BOILS!

GLORP!

AND A TRUCKLOAD OF **SHEEPGUTS!**

SHEEP G'R'US

AND 1000 GALLONS OF **RAW SEWAGE!**

RAW SEWAGE INC.

HA HA HA! SEE YA LATER, **JERK!**

THANK **GOD**, THEY'VE FINALLY LEFT....

NOW I CAN GO HAVE **LUNCH!**

END

EVERY ARTIST GETS A LITTLE BIT BACKED-UP ONCE IN A WHILE! WE GET SO EXCITED THAT THINGS JUST JAM TIGHT! WHEN THAT HAPPENS, WE'LL DO ANYTHING TO REMOVE OUR...
COMPOSER'S BLOCK
STORY BY DENNIS EICHHORN · PENCILS BY PATRICK MORIARITY
INKS BY JIM BLANCHARD ©1991
YOU CALLED FOR MY SERVICES?
YOU SHOULD KNOW THAT I COST ONE HUNDRED DOLLARS, IN ADVANCE.
MABEL WAS TALL, BROWN-HAIRED AND THIN, WITH HER HAIR BOBBED IN A 20'S FLAPPER-CUT. SHE CAME INTO THE APARTMENT LIKE SHE OWNED IT, SIZED ME UP WITH A COOL GLANCE, AND DEFTLY SETTLED HER HANDBAG ON THE PIANO.
YOU WON'T HAVE TO DO MUCH TO EARN IT.
RIGHT NOW, I JUST WANT YOU TO SIT ON MY FACE.
MABEL TUCKED THE MONEY AWAY AND GRINNED.
SQUIRM
NO PROBLEM.
ARE YOU GOING TO TAKE YOUR CLOTHES OFF? AND WHAT SHOULD I CALL YOU?
CALL ME MR. BIG.
I STRIPPED DOWN TO THE BUFF, AND LAID DOWN ON THE KING-SIZED BED.
I'M A MUSICIAN, AND I'VE DEVELOPED A COMPOSER'S BLOCK.
I'M STUCK ON THE LAST STANZA OF MY LATEST COMPOSITION.
DO TELL...
...HOW SHOULD I POSITION MYSELF?

Panel 1	Panel 2	Panel 3

Panel 1: "!" — "LIKE *THIS!*"

Panel 2: SHE WAS SO LIGHT, LIKE A COMPLIANT MANNEQUIN... I TURNED HER AROUND SO THAT HER CUNT WAS RIGHT IN MY FACE, AND HER FACE WAS POINTED AWAY. HER HANDS WERE ON MY KNEES.

"READY, MR. BIG?" "READY. STICK YOUR BOX IN MY FACE, AND *KEEP IT THERE.* GRIND IT AROUND ALL YOU WANT."

Panel 3: "I'LL SLAP YOUR BUTT WHEN I'M READY, AND THEN YOU CAN GIVE ME SOME HEAD. GOT IT?" "GOT IT!"

Panel 4: THEN SHE SMASHED HER CUNT ONTO MY FACE WITH THE FORCE OF A BATTERING RAM. IT WRITHED AND SMOOSHED MY NOSE, MY MOUTH, MY EYES AND CHEEKS AND EARS, MY CHIN AND FOREHEAD. IT WAS LIKE A LIVING THING, WITH A FAINT SCENT OF LILACS AND A DASH OF COCONUT IN THE JUICES. AH, THE JUICES! THE TASTE! IT FLOWED FROM THAT PULSATING CUNT LIKE THIN HONEY, AND I BEGAN TO LAP IT UP AND LICK IT AS FAST AS I COULD.

"OoooF"

Panel 5: I GAVE IT EVERYTHING I HAD, RAMMING MY TONGUE INTO EVERY CORNER I COULD FIND, LICKING AND SWALLOWING LIKE A MAN GONE INSANE. THE SMELL OF CUNT WAS EVERYWHERE, STRONG MUSTY PRIMAL STUFF, AND I FELT MY COCK ENGORGING, GETTING READY FOR RELEASE. I FOUND MABEL'S CLIT WHEN HER LABIAL LIPS CRUNCHED ACROSS MY MOUTH, AND I BIT INTO IT AND HELD ON, FEELING HER GRIP TIGHTEN ON MY KNEECAPS.

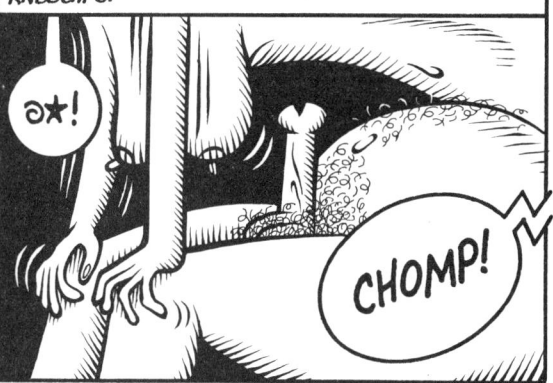

"@★!" "CHOMP!"

Panel 6: SMACK

Panel 7: SHE LOWERED HER HEAD AND TOOK MY ENTIRE PRICK INTO HER MOUTH, ROLLING HER TONGUE AROUND IT AS SHE DID SO. I WAS READY TO COME, AND AS I FLICKED MY TONGUE AGAINST HER TINY IMPRISONED CLIT, I CAME IN MABEL'S MOUTH, GREAT FOAMING GOBS OF SPERM. AS I FINISHED MY IMPASSIONED SPURTS, MABEL RAMMED THE TIP OF HER SHARP TONGUE INTO MY COCK-HOLE, SENDING A SPEAR OF PAIN UP MY GROIN THAT GOT ME HARD AGAIN. AS MABEL RUBBED AND COAXED MY COCK AND BALLS, HER MUFF CONTINUED TO BUMP AND GRIND ON MY FACE.

Panel 8: SLAP — "?!"

I PUSHED MABEL'S CUNT FROM MY FACE AND GOT ON MY KNEES BEHIND HER. I FUCKED HER DOGGIE-STYLE, SPANKING HER HARD ON THE ASS, AND WHEN I CAME FOR THE SECOND TIME, I HEARD BELLS...THEN STRINGS...AND THEN A BASS LINE.

I'VE GOT IT!
IT GOES... 'SHOULD HAVE A CHANCE TO HAVE A DONALD DUCK IRON!'
?
POP
I HUMMED THE MELODY, THEN WENT TO THE PIANO AND PICKED IT OUT. IT WORKED!
WHAT'S THAT?
THAT'S THE REST OF THE TUNE I WAS WORKING ON! IT'S AN ADVERTISING JINGLE FOR THE DONALD DUCK IRON COMPANY! IT GOES... "EVERY SINGLE GIRL IN THE WHOLE WIDE WORLD, SHOULD HAVE A CHANCE TO OWN A DONALD DUCK IIIIIRRRRoooNN!
LIKE IT?
I GUESS SO... ARE WE DONE?
YOU BET WE ARE! YOU CURED MY COMPOSER'S BLOCK, YOU AND YOUR LIVING LEGEND OF A CUNT!
HOPE I DIDN'T SPANK YOU TOO HARD.
I'VE HURT WORSE.
AFTER A WHILE YOU GET USED TO IT.
WELL, MAYBE I'LL SEE YOU AGAIN SOME-TIME.
YOU'VE GOT MY NUMBER.
END

Thanksgiving with MAGGIE BLOODSTONE
CARTOONS- PAT MORIARITY INKS- J. LITTLE
THERE I WAS, HAVING DINNER WITH FOUR OF MY FAVORITE WHITE BOYS: R. CRUMB (HIMSELF), BILL WILLINGHAM (TALENTED SMUT ARTIST), GARY GROTH (PUBLISHER AND FAILED CATHOLIC), AND PATRICK MORIARITY (TOKEN SENSITIVE MALE). THERE ARE FEW THINGS IN THE WORLD I ENJOY MORE THAN BRINGING UP INAPPROPRIATE AND UNAPPETIZING SUBJECTS AT THE DINNER TABLE, SO, CONSIDERING THE COMPANY I WAS IN, I DECIDED THE IDEAL TOPIC FOR DISCUSSION WAS:
HOW COME THERE ARE NO COOL SLANG TERMS FOR FEMALE MASTURBATION?
?
??
!?
!
THERE ARE VIRTUALLY A BAZILLION COLORFUL WAYS OF DESCRIBING MALE ONANISM, INCLUDING:
MUNCH MUNCH
SLURP
"CHOKING THE CHICKEN"
CHOMP MUNCH
CHEW CHEW
"BEATING THE BISHOP"...
BAM BAM BAM
SLURP SIP
"WRINGING THE WEASEL"
AAK
"WAXING THE DOLPHIN"
MUNCH MUNCH MUNCH
"SHOOTING PUTTY AT THE MOON"
HEE HEE
GADS!
DUCK!
"SPANKING THE MONKEY"
HA HA
"POLISHING THE SALAMI"
PLEASE, I'M TRYING TO EAT.
CHOKE GAG
WELL, I GUESS THAT'S THE FAILURE OF FEMINISM: NO GOOD EXPRESSIONS FOR WANKING!
CRUNCH CRUNCH CRUNCH
GARY
AND I THOUGHT:
THAT MAY VERY WELL BE TRUE! *
* MUCH AS I AM LOATH TO ADMIT GARY GROTH BEING RIGHT ABOUT ANYTHING TO DO WITH FEMINISM
IT SEEMS THAT MEN ARE STILL FREE TO WANK TO THE MAX IN PRIVATE--IN GROUPS, EVEN--AND SIMULATE PRIAPIC FRENZY IN PUBLIC.
GLUG GLUG
CHEW CHEW
MUNCH MUNCH SLURP!
...BUT CLITORAL COLLOQUIALISMS ARE IN WOEFULLY SHORT SUPPLY!
I PROCEEDED TO RELATE IN DETAIL MY EARLIEST EXPERIENCES IN FEMALE FLIPPY-FLOPPY:
GASP
AND THEN I...
CHOKE
?!
COUGH COUGH
I THINK A COMMENT ABOUT "MATTED FUR" PROMPTED R. CRUMB TO EXCLAIM:
WHAT A RAUNCHY WOMAN!
BUT DIG: JUST BECAUSE OUR EQUIPMENT DOESN'T SNAP TO ATTENTION OR FLAP IN THE WIND DOESN'T MEAN WE CAN'T INDULGE IN POETIC, FUNNY--YES, AND RAUNCHY HOMAGES TO YONI-WORSHIP! WHY SHOULD WE SETTLE FOR LIMP (AHEM) EUPHEMISMS LIKE "DIDDLE" OR "DRY-HUMP"! THINK WHAT SHEER FEMALE ENERGY THERE IS TO FIND IN PHRASES LIKE "CLAM-DIGGING", "CHERRY-PICKING" (VIRGINS ONLY), AND "RIDING THE NIGHT-MARE!"
MEN JUST DON'T WANT TO ADMIT THAT WOMEN CAN ORGASM WITHOUT THEIR HELP!
END

FUSS ON THE BUS

STORY: DENNIS P. EICHORN
ART: PAT MORIARITY & JIM BLANCHARD

I WAS RUSHING DOWN SEATTLE'S THIRD AVENUE TO CATCH A BUS IN FRONT OF THE POST OFFICE, WHEN I SAW IT PULL AWAY FROM THE CURB A FEW FEET AND THEN STOP...

GOOD! IT'S GOT TO WAIT FOR THAT RED LIGHT!

FOR SOME REASON, THE DRIVER WOULDN'T LET ME BOARD.

HEY! OPEN THE DOOR!

THE LIGHT TURNED GREEN, AND THE BUS MOVED OFF.

WHAT BULLSHIT! FUME! FUME!

I'LL JUST 'JOG' UP TO THE NEXT STOP AND GET ON THERE!

HEAVY TRAFFIC

WHEN THE BUS ARRIVED AT THE NEXT STOP ON PIKE STREET, I WAS READY AND WAITING.

HUFF PUFF

?!

NEITHER THE DRIVER NOR I SAID ANYTHING...

...WE DIDN'T NEED TO.

I WENT TO THE BACK OF THE BUS AND FOUND A SEAT. EVERY TIME I LOOKED TOWARD THE FRONT, I SAW THE DRIVER'S EYES GLARING AT ME IN THE REAR-VIEW MIRROR.

40

BY THE TIME WE GOT TO MY STOP ON FIFTEENTH AVENUE, THE BUS WAS HALF EMPTY. AS I PAID MY FARE, I COULD SENSE THE DRIVER'S ANGER.
ZIP!
ESPRESSO
?
OK... LET'S GET TO IT.
? ? ?
WHA...?
WHY YOU... GET BACK ON THIS BUS AND I'LL KICK YOUR ASS!
LOOK! THEY'RE GOING TO FIGHT!
WHO?
THE BUS DRIVER AND THAT LONG-HAIRED GUY!
YOU COME HERE.
PUNCH HIM OUT!
KNOCK HIS TE LOOSE
I'LL KILL YA MOTHER FUCKER!
FIVE BUCKS ON THE BLACK GUY!
THUMP THUMP
TALK'S CHEAP.
DRIVER! WHAT'S THE HOLD UP?
GRRRR.....
GRIND!
CHICKENSHIT!
BOOOO! HE'S LEAVING!
COME ON, FIGHT LIKE A MAN!
YAAAAAAY!!!
THE BIG WEINER!
THAT FUCKER NEVER EVEN GAVE ME A TRANSFER!
WHAT A LETDOWN!
KICK
END

FRANK LLOYD WRIGHT IS *SO* MUNDANE.

BY PAT MORIARITY & ART PENN

MY DAD, A REAL ESTATE INVESTOR, SENT ME TO STUDY ARCHITECTURE AT THE UNIVERSITY OF WASHINGTON HERE IN SEATTLE, WHERE THE *REAL* MASTERS OF DESIGN HAVE LEFT THEIR MARK...

...LIKE THE *INNER-CITY ANTIQUE TREEHOUSE!* IT'S PERCHED ATOP A TREETRUNK IN CAPITOL HILL AND WAS BUILT AROUND THE TURN OF THE CENTURY— BY A *ONE-ARMED JUDGE!*

ALSO, THERE'S *THE SHOWBOAT THEATER*, WHICH LOOKS LIKE A BOAT FLOATING IN THE CANAL, SOUTH OF THE U.W. IT'S SAID TO BE *HAUNTED* BY THE GHOST OF AN ACTOR, AND IS SCHEDULED FOR DEMOLITION SOON. SEE IT WHILE YOU CAN!

THEN WE HAVE *THE WALKER ROCK GARDEN*, A MOVING TRIBUTE TO WHAT ONE MAN CAN ACCOMPLISH WITH TRUCKLOADS OF PEBBLES AND A *WHOLE LOT* OF SPARE TIME!

NEED TO DRAW ATTENTION TO YOUR BUSINESS? ADORN THE PLACE WITH A *LIFE-SIZE ELEPHANT!* IT WORKS!

ELEPHANT Super CAR WASH
616 Battery St.

Aurora Flower Shop
8808 Aurora N.

THE *HAT AND BOOTS* IS ONE OF SEATTLE'S MOST FAMOUS LANDMARKS, THOUGH IT'S NOW ABANDONED AND IN EXTREME DISREPAIR. THE LESSER KNOWN *TOP HAT BUILDING* CROWNS A HIGH HILL IN THE (YOU GUESSED IT) TOP HAT DISTRICT, NORTH OF BURIEN. ORIGINALLY A RESTAURANT, THE BIG CHAPEAU CURRENTLY SHELTERS A TRANSMISSION REPAIR SHOP.

TOP HAT

Hat n' Boots

THEY'RE ALL SO WONDERFUL, I COULDN'T DECIDE WHICH ONE I LIKED BEST... SO DAD'S GOING TO BUY THEM *ALL*!

P-I
LATTE
TOE TRUCK
14 ROY ST.
ESPRESSO

PROOF

Being an editor has its moments. Take the time Mink and Peggy dropped by, for instance...

"Now, what happened?"

"We were out fishing on the sound between Burien and Vashon Island..."

"...just killing some time, catching a few rays, having a couple beers."

"It was a nice day, and Mount Rainier was looking good, so I took out our camera and snapped a picture of it, amoung others."

SIP
SPLKK!

"It took us a few days to finish that roll of film. Peggy developed it in our darkroom at home."

"What's this?!"

"Look, Mink... two specks in the sky. I don't remember seeing anything like THAT when I took the picture!"

"Me neither."

44

NATURALLY, I WAS CURIOUS. I MADE AN ENLARGE-MENT, FOCUSING ON THE SPECKS. AND GUESS WHAT THEY TURNED OUT TO BE?
WHAT?
ANGELS?
DUCKS?
FLYING SAUCERS?
NONE OF THE ABOVE. IT WAS A SMALL AIRPLANE...
...DROPPING WHAT LOOKED LIKE...
A BODY IN A CHAIR!
WHAT?!
A BODY IN A CHAIR?
GASP!
THAT'S RIGHT! IT LOOKED LIKE SOME-BODY HAD DUMPED A BODY IN THE PUGET SOUND, BETWEEN SEATTLE AND TACOMA!
WE CALLED THE POLICE RIGHT AWAY.
SIGH
THEY SAID TO SIT TIGHT AND WAIT. WITHIN AN HOUR, TWO FBI AGENTS ARRIVED.
RED DRESS
THEY QUESTIONED US, AND SEIZED THE PRINTS AND NEGATIVES.
WE'LL JUST TAKE THOSE AS EVIDENCE.
IF YOU KNOW WHAT'S GOOD FOR YOU, YOU'LL FORGET THIS EVER HAPPENED.
GRAB!
THE AGENTS TOLD US NOT TO TALK TO ANYBODY AT ALL ABOUT THIS. THEY WARNED US WE COULD GET INTO **BIG TROUBLE** IF WE EVER DID.
SO WHY ARE YOU TELLING **ME** ABOUT IT **NOW?!**
BECAUSE IT HAPPENED OVER TWO YEARS AGO, AND WE'VE NEVER HEARD ANYTHING MORE ABOUT IT. THAT DOESN'T SEEM RIGHT TO US.
TOO BAD THE FBI TOOK THE EVIDENCE. NOW YOU CAN'T PROVE WHAT YOU SAY IS TRUE.
YES WE CAN.

"I MADE ANOTHER PRINT BEFORE THE AGENTS CAME. HERE IT IS..."

"SEE?"

"YOU'RE RIGHT. IT'S HARD TO ARGUE WITH **THIS.**"

END

STORY-DENNIS P. EICHHORN / CARTOONS-PAT MORIARITY / INKS-JIM BLANCHARD ©1993

ON THE ROAD
WITH THE
GOOPS
HEFFMAN
VLAD
EL
BASS PLAYER OF THE WEEK
SCREEECH!!!
OH LOOK! IT'S THE GOOPS!
?!
DEAR GOD!
KILL
©1994 PAT MORIARITY & JIM BLANCHARD
SPRONG!
CHECK THIS OUT, HEFFMAN...
SPECIAL GUEST DENNIS
HOP!
BOUNCE!
KILL
...SINCE THE RAMONES HAVE BEEN PLAYING, THE NEEDLE HASN'T EVEN MOVED! IT TOOK UNDER A QUARTER TANK TO GET TO NEW HAVEN! I'M TELLING YOU, THIS IS THE RAMONE-MOBILE. IT RUNS ON RAMONE ALONE!!
DUDE, THIS IS EL AND THE BASS PLAYER OF THE WEEK.
...OH, AND THERE'S VLAD AND HEFFMAN.
GO OUT, DEEPER...

TOSS!
BEER
BASH!
LOOK WHAT I FOUND!
COOL!
PITCH IT BABY
FLING!
PITCH IT!
HA HA
SPLORCH!
ALRIGHT!
EEEEEWW!
PLOP!

49

TOSS!
HEY YOU GUYS!!! YOU GOTTA CHECK OUT THE BATHTUB UP HERE! IT'S REALLY NICE, AND BIG!
BATH. BATHTUB... BATHTIME! LET'S GO!
GRUMBLE GRUMBLE
NICE HUH?
YEAH, I REALLY THINK I NEED A BATH!
SPLASH
C'MON IN
WOOOO!
HA
SPLASH!
OH SHIT, WHAT'S GOING ON HERE?
FUCK OFF AND GET US SOME WATER TOYS!

I NEED A BEER. SOMEBODY GET ME A BEER!
BEER! BEER! BEER AND WATER TOYS!
GET YOUR TOE OUT OF MY ASS!
PSSSSS
HEY MARK, YOU BETTER COME CHECK THIS OUT! THERE'S A BUNCH OF FREAKS IN YOUR DAMN BATHTUB!
HA HA HA HA HA HA HA HA HA HA HA HA HA HA HA HA HA
LOAF
CLICK!
NO PICTURES!
SPLASH! SPLASH!
YIKES!
HEY YOU GUYS, COME ON!
WE'RE GONNA BE LATE FOR SOUND-CHECK.

FUCK SOUNDCHECK!
WE DON'T NEED NO STINKING SOUND CHECK!
BUD
BONK!
FUCK YOU.
JERK!
AAAAIIEE! TH-THAT'S C-C-COLD!
G-GG..
L-L-L- L-LL...
LEAP!
THERE GO THE GOOPS.
SIGH
TO THE GIG!

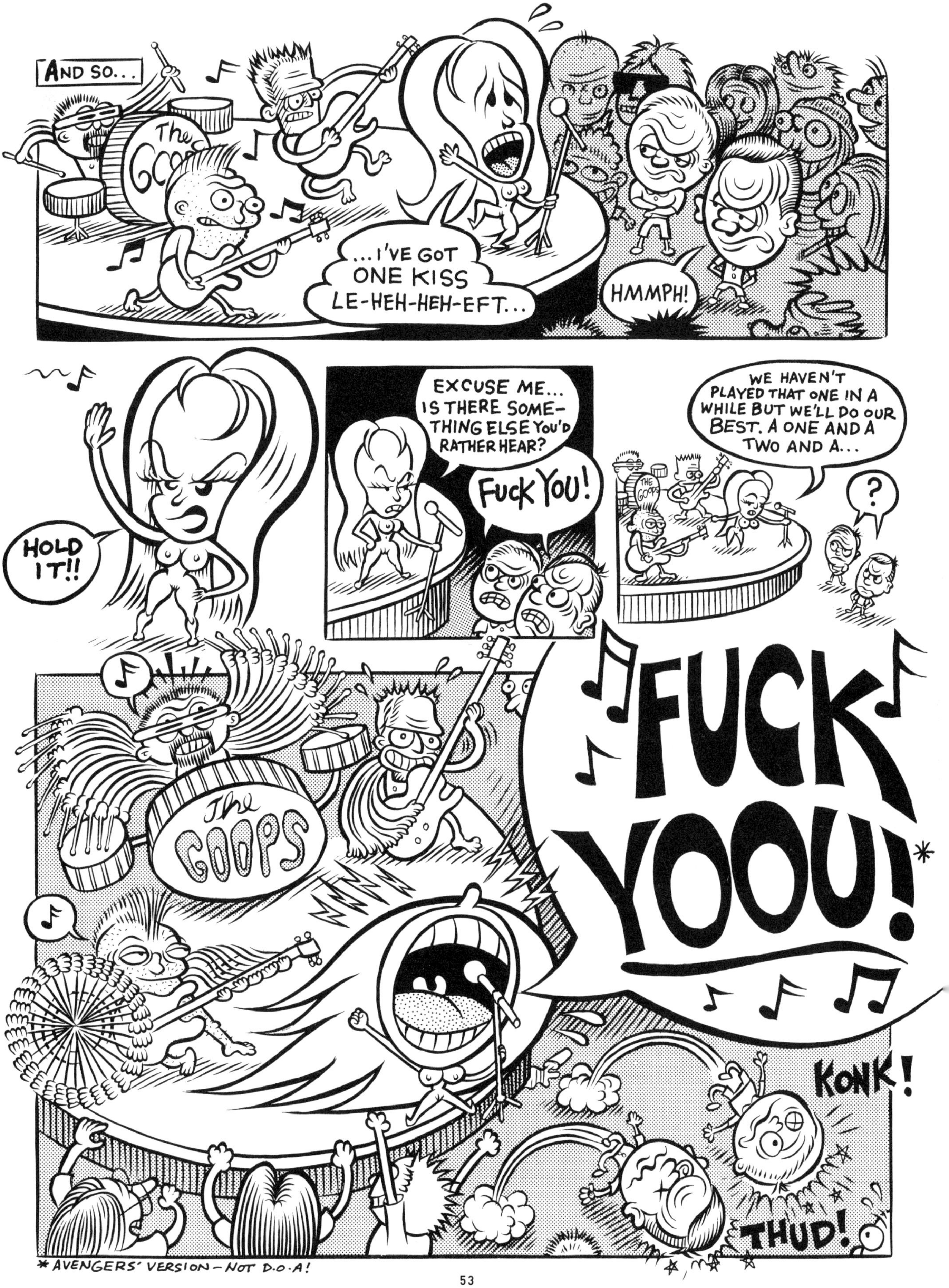

* AVENGERS' VERSION – NOT D.O.A!

THE GOOPS RELAX BACKSTAGE...
KNOCK! KNOCK!
CREEEK!
AN OFFERING...
BARF!
BEER
PLOP!
END

CELEBRITY CAR CRASH CORNER
HE WAS THE MARLBORO MAN OF ABSTRACT PAINTING. HIS MACHO IMAGE WAS AS INFLUENTIAL AS HIS ART. HE HAD THE BROODING MOODYNESS OF KURT COBAIN... THE CIGARETTE DANGLING HIP OF JAMES DEAN. HE WAS A STUD: HE WAS
JACKSON POLLOCK
1912-56
HE WAS BORN ON A WYOMING SHEEP RANCH. AS A YOUNG HANDSOME ATHLETIC MAN, HE BROUGHT VIOLENT INTENSITY TO THE NEW YORK ART SCENE... USING HIS "CONTROLLED ACCIDENT" STYLE OF PAINTING....
THAT HUNK IS A PAINTER?
HE'S ENGAGING THE CANVAS
NO, IT'S SUPPOSED TO BE 2-D!
...A STYLE SO RADICALLY DIFFERENT THAT HE WAS ANOINTED LEAD PAINTER OF HIS GENERATION!
HE'S THE GREATEST SINCE PICASSO
HE IS AS HANDSOME AS GARY COOPER!
RESPECTED ARTS PATRON PEGGY GUGGENHEIM
POLLOCK HAD A HARDER TIME CONTROLLING WHAT HAPPENED OFF THE CANVAS....
PAINTING IS NO PROBLEM.
THE PROBLEM IS WHAT TO DO WHEN YOU'RE NOT PAINTING.
JACKSON HAD BEEN A HEAVY DRINKER SINCE HIS TEENS. HE WAS TREATED FOR ALCOHOL ABUSE. HE RECEIVED EXTENSIVE PSYCHIATRIC COUNSELING THROUGHOUT HIS ADULT LIFE....
I BELIEVE I DETECT AN UNDERLYING SCHIZOPHRENIA...
...BUT, ALAS, THEY JUST COULDN'T BREAK THROUGH HIS SILENT, SELF-PITYING RESISTANCE.
THE OVERWHELMING ACCLAIM AND CELEBRITY TREATMENT DIDN'T HELP EITHER. IT ONLY MADE POLLOCK EVEN MORE SELF-CONSCIOUS... ALMOST TO THE POINT OF ARTISTIC PARALYSIS.
EVEN HIS LONG ISLAND STUDIO WAS NO LONGER A REFUGE.
BY THE EARLY 50'S HE'D BEEN MARRIED, WITH SEVERAL MISTRESSES. HE GRADUALLY GOT UP TO DRINKING A CASE OF BEER A DAY. POLLOCK WAS SOON IN A SERIES OF "UNCONTROLLED ACCIDENTS."
LET ME OUT!
SLOW DOWN, JACKSON! THERE'S A CURVE AHEAD!!
(HIC!)
THEY WEREN'T PRETTY.
PAT MORIARITY

MR. STATISTIC
MOVES TO SEATTLE
WRITTEN, DRAWN, AND INKED BY
PAT MORIARITY (WOW!) ©1993
SOB
PUP
BOOT!
SORRY CHARLIE! YER OFF THE LABEL! NOT ENOUGH GRUNGE, I GUESS! HA HA HA HA
I HATE THIS TOWN!
KONK!
"GRUNGE"... HMMMPH! WHAT THE HELL DOES "GRUNGE" EVEN MEAN?!... SOME MUSIC SCENE! I MUST HAVE BEEN OUT OF MY MIND FOR BUYING ALL OF THAT SEATTLE HYPE!..* SIGH *... ...MAN, EVERYTHING ABOUT THIS TOWN IS REALLY STARTING TO GET ON MY NERVES... BIG TIME!
SKIP
LATTE?
HAPPY GO LATTE
POW!
HAPPY GO LATTE
I AM SO SICK OF COFFEE...BLACKENED SALMON... "ALTERNATIVE" WEEKLIES... MICRO BREWS...NIRVANA... ...ALTERNATIVE MUSIC... ...JUNKIES...MONSTER BURGERS... ALTERNATIVE COMIC BOOKS... ALTERNATIVE SHMIRNATIVE!
WHY, OH WHY DID I LEAVE (YOUR TOWN HERE)?
RUMBLE! RUMBLE!
POUR!
FRANTICS
WAILERS
VICEROYS
DYNAMICS
SONICS
MAGIC FERN
TOM, THUMB & THE CASUALS.
DON & THE GOOD TIMES
DAILY FLASH
PAUL REVERE & THE RAIDERS
CHROME CIRCUS
THE BARDS
BLUE BIRD

OH YEAH... IT WAS THE WEATHER...
GOD, I'M SO DEPRESSED
DROPPED FROM SOB PUP RECORDS, FIRED FROM ESPRESSORAMA, AND BANNED FROM THE BLUE MOON, ALL IN ONE DAY!... I DON'T THINK I COULD STAND LIVING ANOTHER MINUTE IN THIS SO CALLED "EMERALD CITY" ... BUT I'M TOO BROKE TO LEAVE! I WANT TO DIE... RIGHT NOW! ...BUT HOW?
OF COURSE! SEATTLE'S SPACE NEEDLE! HOW PERFECT! HOW POETIC! I'M GONNA GO IN STYLE!
HA HA HA HA HA
SICK LAUGH
RESTAURANT OR OBSERVATION DECK?
WHATEVER'S ON TOP.
TICKETS
NOW TO JUST SQUEEZE THROUGH THESE WIRES AND....
GASP!
...'SCUSE ME WHILE I KISS THE SKY!
?!!
SOB PUP
CRASH!
IS HE.... DEAD?
...YES! SIGN HIM BACK ON! RECORD SALES WILL GO THROUGH TH' ROOF!
THE HAPPY END!
JUNIOR CADILLAC
BIG HORN
GRAND THEFT AUTO
THE HEATS
THE DUCKY BOYS
THE SHEMPS
THE LIMP RICHARDS
GITS
BLOOD CIRCUS
HAMMER-BOX
MOTHER LOVE BONE
GREEN RIVER
NIRVANA

WRITTEN BY EICHHORN PENCILED BY MORIARITY INKED BY BLANCHARD LETTERED BY CRABB ©95

HOW THE COMICS JOURNAL GETS MADE:
SMOKIN' SECTION
IT GETS MADE IN THERE... REALLY!
PAT MORIARITY COMICS JOURNAL "INSIDER"
STAGE ONE: GET A BIG NEWS STORY
HELLO THERE. THIS IS DOUG OGG, NEWS EDITOR AT THE COMICS JOURNAL. I WAS JUST WOND—
THE COMICS JOURNAL?! LISTEN, PUNK! YOU CAN JUST TELL THAT GARY G HE CAN G
NEWS BIG TIME DISTRIBUTOR INSULTS GROTH
STAGE TWO GATHER TOGETHER STORIES, INTERVIEWS AND REVIEWS.
BEING A NEW MANAGING EDITOR AND ALL, YOU MAY NOT BE AWARE OF THIS, BUT THE REAL REASON I KEEP GETTING NEGATIVE REVIEWS IN THE COMICS JOURNAL IS BECAUSE FANTAGRAPHICS IS CONSPIRING AGAINST ME! BUT, HOO-BOY!! WILL THEY BE SORRY WHEN MY NEW COMIC "ZITFACE: REVENGE IS MINE" SOARS TO THE TOP OF THE CHARTS PROBABLY STEALING READERS FROM HATE...
GAWD! JUST ANSWER THE QUESTION! PUH-LEEZ!
STAGE THREE: TRANSCRIBE ALL RECORDED MATTER INTO USABLE COMPUTER DATA.
STUPID MACHINE! FUCK YOU!
OUTDATED 1970s COMPUGRAPHIC TYPESETTING EQUIPMENT
"ALL CARTOONISTS EVENTUALLY"
GROSS CHEMICALS THAT MAKE US ILL...
TAP TAP
STAGE FOUR: SELL ADS.
YOU GOT IT!
ISSUE 159 ROCKS!
HUH? WHUZZAT? YOU'RE IN?!!
GREAT! REMEMBER— WE RULE. THEY SUCK.
STAGE FIVE: TYPESET ALL COPY ACCORDING TO OFFICIAL COMICS JOURNAL SPECIFICATIONS.
GODDAMN COMPUGRAPHIC MOTHERF...
FUCK YOU, FUCK YOU, FUCK YOU!
CLICK TAP CLACKITY CLACK CLACK CLACK TAP TAP
STAGE SIX: LAYOUT & DESIGN.
ZAP!
HOW DO YOU SPELL THIS?
STAGE SEVEN: FINAL ANALYSIS.
U.P.S. MAN IS TEN MINUTES EARLY.!!
TICK
JUST LET IT GO...
CHECK!
WE GOTTA FIX THIS
SHIT!
STAGE EIGHT: PACK UP, TAPE UP, EXPRESS TO PRINTER.
ALMOST READY, MR. U.P.S. MAN!
TICK TICK TICK TICK
SCREEE
GRUMBLE
UPS
STAGE NINE: GARY EDITS.
OY VEY!
HOLD IT RIGHT THERE...
DARKHORSE PUBLISHES GOOD COMIC
NEVER THE END
© PAT MORIARITY 1990

Devil Stay Away from Me

Devil, stay away from me
Devil, won't you let me be?
I don't like you anymore
You're not welcome at my door
Jesus died to save my soul,
Evil is the Devil's goal,
To the Savior this I Pray
Keep the Devil far away

WRITTEN BY J.R. WILLIAMS DRAWN BY PAT MORIARITY INKED BY EARL CRABB! © 1994

KARMIC KEGLING
BY DENNIS P. "MR. 189" EICHHORN AND PAT MORIARITY ©96
BÖLVS ANGIPORVM
DRIVE-IN
LIQUOR
POOL
MARLBORO
SOME FOLKS ARE FAR TOO EAGER TO DIS BOWLING!
LET'S TRUNDLE ORBS, MOTHERFUCKERS
DÉCLASSÉ!
TRÈS GAUCHE!
C'EST BOURGEOIS!
THEY DON'T REALIZE THAT THEY'RE PASSING UP A TRULY TRANSCENDENTAL EXPERIENCE!
PAIR OF SIZE 13s, PLEASE.
THAT'LL BE ONE DOLLAR
SHOES
BOWL RENO
FIRST OFF, BEFORE THE GAME BEGINS, THE "TABULA" IS TOTALLY "RASA".
ANYTHING IS POSSIBLE...
LET'S ROLL!
AS SOON AS YOU HURL THE FIRST SPHERE, THE FUTURE BEGINS TO UNFOLD... AND IF YOU GET A STRIKE IN THE FIRST FRAME...
MEIN GOTT!
MON DIEU!
CRASH!
...THEN THE POTENTIAL FOR A PERFECT GAME EXISTS!
ONLY ELEVEN MORE STRIKES AND I'LL HAVE A SCORE OF 300!!
SOB
AND, IF YOU DON'T KNOCK ALL THE PINS DOWN WITH YOUR FIRST CAST OF THE GLOBE...
HOPE SPRINGS ETERNAL!
...THEN THERE'S ALWAYS THE SECOND BALL...
ALLAH BE PRAISED!
CRASH!
...AND INSTANT REDEMPTION!
SURE, IT'S ALWAYS A TEMPTATION TO UNLEASH YOUR AGGRESSION...
EAT SHIT AND DIE ASSHOLES!
UMPH!
ANOTHER HARMLESS THUNDER-BOLT...
YAWN
CLUNK!
...BUT THIS SELDOM ACHIEVES THE DESIRED RESULT.

JUST REMEMBER, NOT EVERY SPECIES CAN GO BOWLING!
I KEGGLE... THEREFORE I AM!
?
YOU NEED AN OPPOSABLE THUMB TO DO IT PROPERLY!
YEP, THIS PASTIME HAS GOT IT ALL!
SHORT-TERM-GOAL FULFILLMENT...
STRIKE!
...AN IDEAL TO PURSUE...
THE BEST IS THE ENEMY OF THE GOOD!
...AND OCCASIONAL PATHOS!
GUTTER-BALL
OOOPS
BONK!
AFTER ALL, BOWLING IS AN ANTIHEROIC ENDEAVOR!
SPLIT!
...AND THAT'S FORTUNATE, BECAUSE THERE'S A TRAGEDY WAITING FOR EVERY HERO!
FINALLY, AFTER ALL IS SAID AND DONE:
189? WHO'D A THUNK IT?
256!
KEGLER, KNOW THYSELF!

POOP
KER SPLASH!
GRUNT!
FLUSH!
I DON'T KNOW WHY I EVEN BOTHER TO EAT CORN...
©P. MORIARITY

DIG THE NEW BREED
P. MORIARITY © 96
DING DONG!
?!
?
GOOD CAUSE CANDY BARS $5
™

65

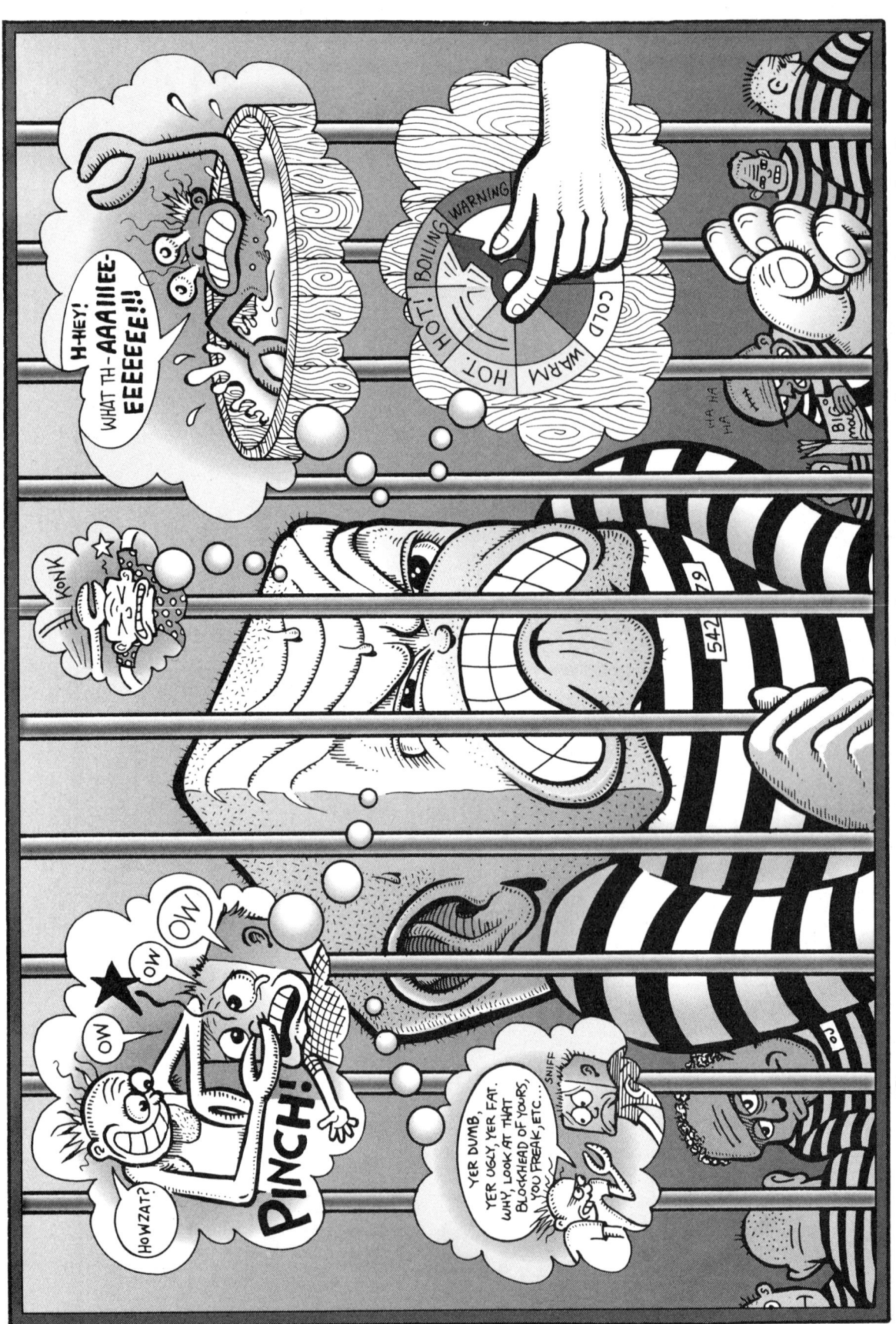

OCT. 15TH, 1994 – Sideshow attraction "The Human Blockhead" receives life in prison for arranging murder of his clawhanded stepfather, "Lobster Boy."

(To inmates: please take it easy on the Human Blockhead – Pat Moriarity '95)